Containment Web

C.K. Malavasic

Published by C.K. Malavasic, 2022.

Copyright

Also by C.K. Malavasic

Siren's Score
Containment Web

Watch for more at https://ckmalavasic.com.

Dedication

To those relatives and friends who encouraged a young author to write fantastical tales but aren't here to see one published. They laid the foundation for this book.

To the relatives, teachers, and friends who graciously stepped into this adventure, learning new skills and techniques along the way and seeing this through.

For those readers who will pick up this work and slip into the world within.

CONTAINMENT WEB

Chapter 1

Space Station

Agata scowled at the medbay containment room, her Hispanic features set in a harsh scowl that would have been equally at home in ancient Mexico as it was on the space station circling the Polaris sun in 2218.

Blowing out a breath, she looked up at her partner, Lorth, "The Wolven or the Skitters?"

Lorth tapped his eight spacesuit-sheathed legs on the floor unhappily, his spider face unmoving but for his mandibles quivering in and out beneath the transparent visor. The translator module inserted in her ears provided his words, "Neither. He let a Ghranthir lay its offspring in his sexual organ, replacing his own sperm. At least we found him before he got off station and started giving human women unexpected babies. I believe it would be like the cuckoo but worse."

Agata shook her head, "I am almost to the point of banning Ghranthir from these sort of interactions. Idiots."

Lorth tapped gracefully on the keyboard they both used, adding medical notes to the file of the unfortunate human, "So am I. I'll bring it to the chief med officer at the next weekly meeting."

"May need to get this spread to all the other space stations. Not worth the forty hour parasite cleanse to cover these dimwits, nor the cost to inventory every time it happens," she stalked over to the the appointment book, "Three more appointments for our shift, one is remote. Ten minutes until the next."

Lorth walked, raising his body slightly to brush the top of her head with his abdomen and moving ahead of her. She was grateful she stood barely over five feet tall. It made it easier for him to move around her, unlike the other med pairs.

Rubbing her neck, fingers brushing over the bumps where the skin-tight spacesuit she wore stretched over the nasty ridged scar covering her nape, she walked after him.

If Lorth hadn't been as fast as he was, she'd have died five months ago from the wound the scar formed from. She shivered, fighting off the images promising to bury her in nightmares yet again.

She knew what a Zinxir was and never wanted to see one again.

Lucky for humanity, they allied with Lorth's species, Aqu-jio, instead of the Zinxir at first contact. If they had switched, humanity would have been wiped out entirely in a few months.

"How is our newest mom?" she peeked in the farthest room from the main bay, reading the monitors with a glance easily.

"She'll take longer to recover, but her child is doing well," Lorth replied from the main room, "Her captain visited earlier. He's limited to two more days before he has to take off. Tomorrow will determine if she and the child are going, or will be staying here."

The armored plating of the mother moved slightly as she breathed, a constant rasping sound filling the room as the plates rubbed against each other. The baby curled into a ball in the crib beside her, the medical devices reading was much improved since last Agata checked.

She agreed with Lorth's assessment. The mother was the one they needed to observe longer as the baby could go on the next transport. He could wear a baby spacesuit without issue.

"Is the final assessment in the appointment book for morning shift?" She asked as she returned to the main room.

Lorth's reply made her frown in concern, "I entered it with highest priority. I hope her improvement continues through the night. It is better for them both to return home so they can perform the rituals of new bonds on their home-world. Our religious envoys are not prepared for such on this station."

"Is there one on a nearby station who could help if they have to stay? I know the Cirthars require this to be performed as soon as possible if they are unable to return home within their timeframe."

"I checked and unfortunately there is none nearby. We'd have to offer an imperfect solution that could cause honor strife later for the baby."

Agata sighed, "Not much we can do right now. If it comes down to it, she may decide to press forward so that bonding can occur per protocol. Is there anything we can do to hand off her care so she's likely to survive the journey better?"

Lorth chuckled, "I have already consulted with the expert and prepared the plan. We are as prepared as we can be. Ah, our appointment has arrived."

The shriek of horror made Agata turn, hands reaching for a med bag.

Only to scowl at the human woman backing away from Lorth.

Lorth sighed, "I do believe this one is yours."

Agata strode forward briskly to come between the human and Lorth, recognizing the ill hidden bigotry and demonization of all Aqu-jios this human clung to. Too many humans recoiled from Lorth and his ilk only because they thought spiders were creepy and pests.

They forgot spiders managed the insect populations of Earth to the benefit of humanity.

Agata thanked the first contact team for having an Arachnologist on board for the hydroponic capsules. If that scientist hadn't been there, humanity would have either insulted or ignored the peaceful spider-like race. Maybe even raced into the furry, clawed clutches of the treacherous, murderous Zinxirs instead.

She learned her lesson first hand about assuming all races that looked like earth species were like their counterparts.

"Hello," Agata greeted with a smile, "I'm Medical Officer Morales. May I ask how we can help you today?"

"You only. Not that monster."

Lorth moved slowly out of view, sending a whisper only Agata heard, "I'll check on our inventory status and prepare resupply lists."

Agata forced her smile to remain light and happy, "I can certainly help. Would you like to go to a private room?"

"Anywhere that thing hasn't been."

Agata gestured down the opposite hall, "This way please."

After an hour, Agata fought off a headache as the human woman scurried out the doors as if jaws snapped at her heels.

"Lorth, that appointment is complete," Agata pressed her fingers to the suit covering her forehead, "Mark her down as human only med-staff."

"Already complete," Lorth tapped her shoulder, "Bad news diagnosis?"

"No. She kept asking the same questions over and over again, expecting a new answer each time. She wants to steal a man from another woman by changing her scent to her rival's. I explained that was illegal and we wouldn't perform the operation."

"Thank goodness we have no grey or black market on this station. She'd have it done in less than ten minutes and may need a parasite cleanse," Lorth stretched, his spacesuit easily adjusting around his limbs, "The next patient should be here in a few minutes."

"I hope they have an easier situation that won't leave my head longing for my pillow."

"That reminds me. Did the new pillow help?"

Agata nodded, "Thank you. The pillow certainly supports my neck and shoulders better."

"Good. We need our sleep to keep up with those who come through our doors."

The door opened and another Aqu-jio stepped in, this one smaller than Lorth, with spindly legs.

"Greetings. I have an appointment for my on station physical," a lowering of the whole body to Lorth, then to Agata told her this was an ultra polite Aqu-jio.

Agata did a curtsey which was the closet a human could come to the whole body dip as Lorth mirrored the gesture from the Aqu-jio.

"I am Medical Officer Lorth of Cometspinners via Aqu-jio Prime," Lorth introduced himself.

Agata appended her greeting after his, "I am Medical Officer Agata of Morales via Human Prime."

Most Aqu-jio knew Human Prime meant Earth, since that mirrored Aqu-jio Prime which was their home-world. Mars was known as Human Second, being the second planet humans colonized.

"I am Expedition Scout Jinor of Traplids via Aqu-jio Hundred Thirty-Seven. Is this an opportune time to proceed with my physical?"

"Indeed," Lorth replied, "Would you..."

The door opened and two humans stood behind Jinor, carrying a third between them.

"I'll handle them," Agata recognized the three men, all anti-Aqu-jios.

Lorth nodded, then gestured with his forelegs to the hallway, "Shall we, Jinor?"

"Please."

Agata moved to the three men, then fought back a snarky snap.

The middle man bore a pulsing lump on his chest that clearly meant he'd been playing "Captain Sex" to a Bengarth.

"Gentlemen, please come this way," she knew she'd be going pass shift end with the parasite cleanse on this fool.

Why did men think it was safe to use their genitals with alien species? It only made medical officers such as herself want to lock them all up in a room and force them to watch how the other species on station gave birth, including those that used other species as incubators.

Just like the Bengarths, Ghranthirs, Wolven, Skitters and a hundred others with similar practices.

Keeping her professional face on, she mentally added, *This is why I don't date anyone who's not in medical or command sectors. They just can't avoid jumping into an alien's bed without reading the fine print on how that alien reproduces outside its kin.*

Stepping down the hall, Agata fought sighing at the numbskulls she had to treat.

Chapter 2

Bargain

Alexander coughed, rubbing his chest at the pain radiating with each breath.

The company doctor assured him it wasn't something bad and he needed some bedrest. Soup and fluids as well.

He fought off the dizziness as he stepped off the underground hover train, walking up to the street level. Then a block to reach his home.

Hacking in the bitter cold that assaulted him outside the warm tunnels, he thought back to the negotiations with the Zinxirs.

He'd been told by his mentors Zinxirs would just as soon murder a human than to bargain with them.

Today's session showed they may be more business minded than expected.

They were willing to part with one of their medical cures for only two hundred million indebted humans to become part of their crew.

Of course the company had an overflow of debtors from the last recession and were happy to hand them over for the right to study and backward engineer the priceless cure.

Wondering for a moment what the Zinxirs would use debtors for, he lost his train of thought with his next coughing fit.

"Hey, man!" The person in front of him sent him a glare, "Watch where you're coughing. I don't need any more sick time."

Alexander sneered, smiling toothily at the man, "Bug off. Your immune system needs more work if you are out of sick time this early in the year."

"Fuck off and die," the reply came before the man stalked away muttering.

Reaching his apartment building, Alexander rapped his knuckles on the scan pad.

It registered his unique bio-key from the pico-bots implanted in his hand, opening the door with a soft chime to the foyer of his building.

Moving across the hall to the elevator, letting the door swing shut behind him, he imagined the loads of money he'd get for figuring out how to make a human version of the cure.

Day-dreaming on his future discoveries and promotions, maybe a lucrative book and movie deal, he coughed his way into the elevator, not even covering his mouth.

People needed to be exposed to germs so their immune systems could react to new strains and threats.

Maybe he'd invent a new germ just to give the population a jolt. Then he'd come out with a vaccine to make those he liked immune to it.

He could get the company to fund it. They would love a new money maker in the medicinal area.

They survived the legalities the first and second world countries required by going to a third world country who all the other countries needed for raw materials and trade supplies. It would be so easy to expose the whole world and a good portion of the space trade routes to it very quickly.

Entering his apartment, he never suspected someone already struck upon the same idea and implemented it for a more destructive purpose than he intended.

Chapter 3
Meetings

Agata sat at the table as the dual chiefs of the medical sector spoke to issues and relayed information from the other stations at the end of the week.

They'd already added species to the ban list, like she wanted, earlier in the meeting, so she made notes of new regulations introduced. She most likely would be forced to explain to ignorant and aggressive men they couldn't stick their ding dongs into the first available hole or get fined for the supplies to cure them. After the first time, most learned to avoid the cost. Before then, they would abuse the med staff with verbal and physical attacks to get their way.

The other space faring species acted more cautiously in interactions with others, going so far to have the med staff present for reproduction negotiations and explanations.

"We have one of our metallic based species coming in for physicals next week. All med staff are required to review those policies applicable for them, especially the new vaccinations available for them. They prefer to have their checks on ship, so we'll rotate on board with three pairs for each shift. Agata, Lorth, you'll be in first shift as shift leads."

Agata lowered her whole body in the chair, then straightened, "Understood, Chief of Med Staff Jourth."

The Aqu-jio clattered his approval after Lorth's body lowered, "Please be aware they will be more respectful of Aqu-jios than humans, so adjust your approaches appropriately."

Agata acknowledged the recommendations.

It had only been four decades since humans finally got off their world and came to the attention of the other space-farers. The delay due to political and genocidal policies throughout the 2000s, resulting in the suppression of science underpinning successful space flight, among other areas.

A decade ago, Agata had been doing her internship for becoming a doctor. One that wouldn't have been allowed off world due to her ancestry.

Then, she would never have imagined she'd be millions of light years away from Earth, practicing medicine with countless species coming through the space station, partnered with one of the best practitioners in the known galaxy. At night, she gave gratitude to the universe for the positive vibes she'd received for her life to date.

"A reminder that our seconds in command for medical will be at a conference lasting six months starting in one month. While they are there, Lorth and Agata will be acting as our seconds. All reports need to include all four until Olirth and Jason board ship to leave."

All acknowledged the change.

The meeting was called, allowing the staff to go their separate ways. Lorth walked above her, a common formation for the two of them.

Lorth asked, "I heard you have a suitor."

Agata sighed, "He is not a suitor. He wants to screw all the human women on board to complete his bucket list for this station. I happened to be one name on that list."

"Why not accept his offer? He's been careful to avoid the others on station that would normally eliminate them from your potential list," Lorth's voice filled with concern, "You have been rather anti-social outside the norm for humans to be classified as anti-social."

Agata looked up at his mandibles, unable to see his eyes. He could be teasing her, however, he didn't normally.

"He's eliminated himself from my strident requirements."

"Your requirements limit your suitors to one per million of humans. It's unlikely you'll find a lover if you keep discounting suitors and refuse to return to Human Prime," Lorth clattered, "I wouldn't mind a vacation if you took it to find a suitable partner for your web."

Agata wanted to tell him she had minimal interest in men of her species since they continually stuck their dicks into orifices they shouldn't.

Unfortunately, due to the politics of the 2000s, those like her who didn't want to love the opposite gender, were punished severely. She'd rather be an icy bitch queen than to let stupidity be bred through her by the so called superior gender.

How she wished the history of the 2000s hadn't taken a nose dive into the second Dark Age. They started out well, granting rights to those marginalized, then let fear of the "other" strip those rights back, then remove more for those who were "normal".

Unwilling to explain to Lorth, who may then ask questions which would get her imprisoned, or worse, about humans still getting back to where they should be, she simply replied, "My web is thick so only those with desired traits may join me. My new suitor is caught in the outer layers and ripe for devouring while those who last tried from Human Prime became lost long before spying those webs."

The translated snort let her know he was diverted, "Sounds like Human Prime needs better suitors. Unless you want to try non-human suitors."

"Considering the number of cases I deal with daily, I'll decline the option for interspecies relationships," she shook her head as they returned to their posts, "Besides, I have completed my required reproduction with one offspring."

Lorth chittered with realization, "Daniel, yes?"

"Daniel is my son. He was accepted into the science exchange program as of five years ago," Agata went to the workstation as the med bay filled with their peers.

"Do you know where?"

"No," as she hid the pain of not knowing where her only child worked currently, though grateful she found out before the divorce, she checked the schedule, then turned around, "We are both on lab work for day shift."

"That time already?" Lorth gave an unhappy clatter as they both turned, then travelled down the hallway to the segregated labs, "Lab work was so much easier prior to the removal of half the team to Human Prime."

"Those lab techs were on contract with Patriot Corp, Inc and they decided not to renew," Agata sighed, "Do you happen to know if the Aqu-jio will be sending more of theirs?"

Lorth tapped her shoulder once they were in the Lab, his whisper only for her ears, "My kind are very displeased with that decision, however, they have sent three to aid us."

She whispered lowly, "Something I need to be aware of?"

"They all are human cautious. I will need to be the go between."

Human cautious meant they would need to see proof the human was worth time and effort to accept. Not nearly as bad as anti-human, but still difficult.

Agata curtsied, "I understand. Let me know when I need to change my routine. I rather ease the lab team's integration as soon as they arrive."

"You are far more...considerate of others than most of your kind."

Agata chuckled, "My ex wouldn't agree with that."

"Your ex wasn't even tolerant of our partnership, so his view is discounted as heavily biased."

Agata smiled as she sat down to begin the lab work for the day, easily handing off tasks to Lorth and taking others back.

A public announcement rang out over the intercom, "All human members of the station are required to attend the latest updates at 19:00 tonight. Confirmation of understanding will be tested."

"Here I hoped for a quiet evening with my latest novel," Agata accepted the meeting invite to her calendar with a rap on the screen beside her, her bio-key registering her identity and which calendar to add it to from the station system.

"Which novel are you reading?"

"The one you recommended by Zhunir of Starsnappers via Aqu-jio Two Thousand Eighty-One. I read the first few chapters last weekend and hoped to continue tonight," she replied.

"I will refrain from commenting on it."

She smiled, "That is appreciated, Lorth."

They worked in companionable silence for the rest of the shift.

Chapter 4

Quarters

Lorth waited for the doors to cycle between the space station common areas where space suits were required for all species and the Aqu-jio section.

The quarters were triple reinforced against breaches so their residents could remove the space suits to attend to personal hygiene and other tasks without danger of a vacuum.

His kind could withstand vacuum for up to ten minutes without harm, but the humans could barely handle twenty-seconds. It was why the human sector had ten times the shielding and six times the redundancies.

Grateful for those protections and the medical suites having the same level for the various species he dealt with, Lorth rubbed his mandibles together with contentment.

Stepping into the sector, the door sealing behind him, the picobots in his helmet retracted back to the neck band, allowing the stiff hairs to rise back to their normal positions.

A female Aqu-jio sitting in a web at the entrance chattered, "How was your shift, Lorth?"

"Decent, Shurith. I have a few more biased individuals identified. We'll see if we can educate it out of them, or if they'll go to more rigid areas so they can work best."

"And your partner? Still weaving well?"

Lorth rubbed his mandibles again, "Quite. She's turning into a firm connection in the web. Her ability to identify members of the humans who have inherent issues with others is higher than expected. The data department is very happy."

"Building the web further. Good. The recruiter on Human Prime proved their assessment correct again."

Lorth chittered seriously, "I'm glad we hold her contract to work on this station and not Patriot Corp. They have been making very detrimental choices in the last year."

Shurith gave a darker response, "The little male who's going through the human females is under their contract. Not respectful to his own kind's females. Best keep two eyes on your partner."

Lorth blew out a breath, "He won't have her in his web. She'll devour him rather than take his dubious gifts."

Shurith rubbed her mandibles, "Good. She should eat the undeserving and those lacking appropriate gifts, just like we do."

Lowering his body, he stepped down the hallway towards his web.

Shurith's voice greeted another Aqu-jio entering the section.

Two security Aqu-jios skittered across the ceiling, their thick but low slung bodies hiding their massive strength. They greeted Lorth as they passed him. He returned the salutations.

Tired, Lorth tapped the tip of his leg to the panel, the picobots registering his bio-key.

Once secured in his quarters, he climbed into his personal web, settling down for rest, picking up the meal one of the caretaker Aqu-jio dropped off for him.

Biting into the reusable container, he slurped up the tasty meal. He wondered what human food tasted like with a brief thought, then turned to the entertainment center.

Tapping in to continue the series from Human Second, he watched humans act out a strange and tangled drama. He found himself enamored of their soap operas and the premise of love pentangles and forbidden interests. It showed more about human psychology than they realized.

The societal expectation of monogamy opposed to their desire for open and various relationships fascinated him. He wondered why they both abhorred and fantasized inter-gender lasting relationships. With the multiple options to reproduce now available to them as part of the science shares, humanity could eliminate the drain on their female partners and support families of any combination.

Lorth tapped his legs on his web thoughtfully, pulling up a thought strand he'd had before.

There were members of the humans who sought love with members of the same gender, but were scorned or persecuted for those natural desires. Or so he'd overheard in the social square.

Pausing the show, he typed up a request to the core medical community of the Aqu-jio. Maybe one of the mental doctors had an idea why humanity would limit themselves so.

Genetic diversity could be enhanced with the hundreds of known methods from the species in the web in addition of eliminating many disorders before conception.

Not expecting a reply for several light-dark cycles, Lorth resumed his show and study.

Chapter 5
Outbreak

"I'm at the address. Send me the wellness checks," the police officer boredly exited his vehicle, closing the door.

Frowning at the six listed for the same building, wondering why so many, he walked up to the front entrance. Rapping his knuckles briskly on the entry pad, he stepped inside.

Nice building, clean. He observed the decor with a sweep as he walked to the elevator.

According to the report, the first individual reported himself sick six weeks ago, last contact three days ago by the company who requested the check in.

Sighing at the company name, he wondered if they really cared, or were just pretending for the world leaders and the stock markets.

Glad to be free of their debt stacking policies, the officer exited the elevator and then towards the door he wanted. Perhaps the poor schmuck he was visiting needed extra days off to deal with issues. The company certainly didn't make it easy to get normal time off when they thought you didn't deserve the days you got.

Stopping at the door, he tapped the panel to ring the doorbell.

He heard nothing, a testament to the soundproofing in the building. Much nicer than his digs, where he unwillingly heard the domestic disturbances and private moments a wee bit too easily.

After several minutes, he rapped his knuckles then waited for the personal assistant for the occupant to speak up.

"Greetings. How may I help you today officer?" The throaty female voice replied from the door speaker.

"When was the last time the resident left his apartment?" He asked, opening the report on his tablet.

"Ten days ago, leaving at 2:11 am, returning at 2:24 am, officer."

"When was the last time the door was opened?" He noted the information so far.

"Four days ago at 5:19 pm, officer."

"I am here for a wellness check. Would you verbally inform the resident?"

"One moment please, officer."

He waited, scanning the hallway, noting some doors were sub-standard and out of compliance.

Scowling, he opened a ticket and sent in to the department about the lack of landlord initiative to keep to quality minimums.

"I have informed him, officer, but he seems confused or dazed."

"Show me," he insisted, putting away his mobile device.

The door flickered then displayed video.

Not only dazed or confused, but sick.

"Open the door under infirm protocol," he swore inwardly.

He didn't need this.

Getting thrown up on wasn't the worse thing to happen, but a close second.

He cautiously slid into the apartment.

It stank, like dead body stench.

"Officer entering due to health concern," he called the standard line, "Please come out, sir."

The chatter of teeth against teeth was the last thing he heard before strong arms latch on him and crushed him to death.

Chapter 6

Space Drills

Lieutenant Commander Bronislava "Bron" Julija noted the latest complaint from the human crew as she stood near the spaceship repair bays.

"...they just run all over without respect for us. Their twitchy legs and drooling mandibles are bad enough, but to have them walk over us like we aren't there isn't right!"

Bron opened her mouth to ask for more details when the wall beside them vanished.

She mentally sighed half in relief, half in exasperation as she and all those in the immediate area were sucked into space, twirling and twisting from the force of escaping atmosphere.

Then she bit back a yelp of pain as her shoulder slammed the edge of debris.

Her suit automatically sealed her in, activating emergency beacons and life support as her vision dizzyingly twirled. It also applied pain-relief to her shoulder, which allowed her to focus on her surroundings.

Step one, reduce rotation.

With returning calm, she mentally tapped into the systems to schedule a small rotational burst.

The so slight vent from her spacesuit made an immediate change.

She still flipped head over feet through space, but she could see much clearer.

On the next flip, she looked at the station lights, rolled her eyes.

They flared blue then green meaning a decompression drill was underway.

The Aqu-jio found the best way to train people on dangerous situations was to toss them into a controlled situation and see who did well, who failed, and what needed to be changed.

Bron had been in space with the Aqu-jio long enough to feel this sort of situation as old hat.

Step two, see where the nearest crew member is.

She scanned the starry field, noting locations of the nearest Aqu-jio first, then her fellow humans.

One Hir-zt, a snake-race coiled through the darkness, looking as relaxed as she did as it watched everything with its six eyes.

With supreme disappointment, Bron realized all the other humans flailed about in panic.

She spoke softly, "I can be last."

Her partner, a long legged Aqu-jio with the name Ziz-ka chittered back in her ear with immense wisdom and experience, "Depends on if any of these are starting rehabilitation for space species. You may need to be my link."

Step three, group up for rescue.

His leg stretched out and gripped a human by the back of their suit with ease.

The human stopped fighting.

Bron scowled as she spotted two refusing Aqu-jio help as they offered legs to hold onto, "Tell me where you need me."

The one Ziz-ka caught was more than happy to grab the next human and stop their twisting. While this happened, others slowly linked up, forming threads of crew drifting through space.

Bron watched six Aqu-jio expend extra energy to snatch humans who tumbled further and further from the main group. Then had to control her hatred as they acted like spoiled children as they were brought back to the strands.

She had a moment to relish the slowly forming web, before Ziz-ka reached out and caught her ankle, pulled her backwards.

Reaching out as she'd done dozens of times, she caught the wrist of another human, almost not needing to see them to snag their suit as she swung by.

Sighing mentally at the ridiculous and stand-offish xenophobia of crew who'd been on board long enough to understand outside appearances meant nothing to who an alien was inside, she reached out with her other hand and gripped the ankle of another human.

Step four, wait.

With the web of those they could catch, they drifted further and further from the station. Bron didn't worry.

She had the timing of the rescue crew down to within ten seconds, so she just held onto her humans.

The stars were especially pretty today. Looked like the cloud of dust particles cleared out since last month, leaving the breath-taking vista open to enjoyment.

If only her fellow humans were so keen on observing space as she was.

"How long must we wait?", "Stupid drill", "Drill? This is a drill? This is nothing like a fire drill!", "I think I lost my work pad," and other complaints filled the comm channel.

Unlike most of the crew with her, she didn't need to fill the silence with anything to stay sane.

The firm and grounding grip on her ankle gave her that.

The rescue crew arrived within her ten-second window, making her smile slightly, before she focused on handoff of her two strands to the reaching hands.

She slipped inside while pulling Ziz'ka in with her.

A great feature of space. It took little pulls or tugs to get the whole web into the rescue ship. With time and patience, they all were collected then on their way home.

She'd finalize what she'd add to her report while a medical handled her shoulder. Then hand in her report to the commander on shift.

With that, she should be free to go to the social hexagon for a meal and her routine of watching everyone interact, or not.

Plan in mind, she sat calmly next to Ziz-ka, scanning the faces around her. The Hir-zt coiled under another Aqu-jio, discussing a recent delivery of artifacts from a plague-destroyed civilization who'd been limited to one planet.

Tossing the name of the planet, Xox-xex Prime, to the back of her mind, Bron watched the easy glide of the rescue ship to the dock.

The humans rushed out, snarling at one another.

Bron sighed, shaking her head, "They should just wait their turn."

Ziz-ka gave an amused chortle, "Ah, youth and their immense delusions of grandeur. I'm very glad I was demoted."

Bron turned and hissed urgently, "Don't use demoted! Demoted to humans means we did something very wrong and are being punished. I will not answer another human asking about what you did."

"Promoted is wrong," he laughed, "We demote our wisest to train the youthful for longevity. It's an honor to be demoted to such a position. We promote those who need more experience so they have wisdom when they cycle through."

"Just don't say that among the humans again," she huffed, resisting folding her arms, "I spent ten hours, ten hours," She repeated in frustration, "of my off-day yesterday explaining you are using the wrong damn word."

The Hir-zt snorted, "I sympathize. They use odd phrases for mating compared to my kind. Ensnare your mate in your webs so they never leave? Then who will get the food for the young and carry the excrement out?"

Bron shook her head, "It's baffling to us as well. The woman stays home and cares for the little one while the man goes for food and shelter."

"You don't alternate?" The Hir-zt uncoiled, "Your women use many resources to bring child to birth, yes? Unfair only she raise while exhausted."

Bron wisely spouted the common line as she stood and walked behind the Hir-zt, "Women are best suited for keeping the young alive as we give milk as their food while they are weak."

"One of those who tend young a while until they leave nest, yes?" At her confirmation, the Hir-zt swayed back and forth in excitement, "Still, woman benefit from leaving nest for some time. Restore her resources, take break, rebalance. Not healthy staying in place."

Bron knew it well from her own mother, "I agree more time for breaks is needed as well as better health care. There is an ancient saying from my people, 'It takes a village to raise a child' and I can attest to the benefits of such thinking."

After all, her mother had slipped too far into her postpartum depression to be brought back. Her village raised her while her mother wasted away.

"You have access to our help," the Hir-zt tapped its tail on her ankle, a supportive gesture and a sign of respect, "We have good incubators that can help ease burden."

"I'm sure our medical staff have researched all options. Two are writing dissertations on using advance techniques for infertile pairs," Bron gave thanks she listened to the medical prattle.

Hir-zts loved talking with other species and considered species with multiple disciplines to be ideal. That or a close social connection to know who had a desired discipline.

"I will check on social web. They may be good discussions. Good form on drill," it complimented her before it slithered away, swaying more in its excitement.

Ziz-ka touched Bron's shoulder, "Medical available now."

Bron nodded before marching over to the lines checking over those who'd been tossed into space.

Several minutes later she was released with a follow-up apportionment in a week.

Ziz-ka moved in tandem with her, his legs ahead and behind her so they walked side by side.

Bron envied Agata's shorter stature as she could walk under her partner. If someone distracted Ziz-ka, he unconsciously adjusted his steps such she had to slow down.

Grabbing a new pad as they passed a station, she rapped her knuckles to bring up her stored data.

All of it was there from before the drill.

Finishing the report, she saved it along with recommendations from her view. All other humans needed remedial lessons ASAP.

Ziz-ka slipped through to the command hallway.

She paced him, a stray thought on if humanity matured enough she'd be able to have children without risking her own life.

The commander pair collected the reports, then let her and Ziz-ka off-duty as per standard post-drill procedures.

They descending deep into the station to the social hexagon where they could get food and mingle.

Bron preferred to watch all the interactions from a wall table.

As they stepped in, a weird hissing alternated from deep to high-pitched started.

Bron blinked as the security Aqu-jio converged on a rather large female Aqu-jio towering over a cowering male Aqu-jio.

The 'bartender' of the social hexagon prepped something at a speed so dizzying, she almost missed it sliding to a stop right next to the female Aqu-jio. The bartender moved back, nine of her twelve eye stalks on the Aqu-jio.

At the same instant, the security Aqu-jio split into two groups, the females circling the towering female, their hums vibrating the air as they moved up and down in an odd dance-like motion, front legs raised. The males gripped the trembling male and hauled him physically away from the female group.

"Overwork," Ziz-ka shivered.

"Overwork?" Bron asked, watching the security team's hum rise and fall in a soothing rhythm in counter-point to the hissing.

"Jo-Ria tends to become engrossed in her work to the point she forgets to sleep or eat. Sometimes both. When female Aqu-jio stress their bodies too much, we males look very tasty. It's why males always offer large packages of nutritious and delicious food as part of their courting. Less likely to lose a limb or head," Ziz-ka gave a noise that made the trembling male scurry into the opposite hall followed by half the male security team, "Hirith is very new to this station and didn't pay caution to Jo-Ria's state. He'll learn."

"The hissing was a threat display?"

Ziz-ka shook with his snort, "That was a combination of 'I'll eat you' and 'I'm pissed' which means dead male. It's why I stayed over here. I've heard and seen its prelude enough times to stay clear," he raised his voice, "Lorth! Jo-Ria again."

Lorth ambled in, Agata carrying a large case under his legs.

Jo-Ria's hissing rose again, making all the male Aqu-jio slide back, including Ziz-ka and Lorth.

Agata strode forward, making Bron tense before Ziz-ka placed a leg in front of her.

A new humming noise joined the female Aqu-jio.

Jo-Ria's head cocked, focused on Agata, the mandibles slowing as did the hissing.

Bron's jaw dropped as Agata joined the dancing circle, her body swaying back and forth, her hum merging with the rest.

"Lorth, you didn't tell me your partner could speak our language so well," Ziz-ka's soft chide drew Bron's gaze away from the memorizing dance.

"She is picking up bits of it. She did so well with the Cizzzirtiz they thought she'd been raised by us. She acted like an Aqu-jio among them, treating me so respectfully they asked if I was her parent."

"Being metallic based, they don't like non-metals save for us and the Kolbirr Hives," Ziz-ka cocked his head, "Her hum has a lesser range than ours, but blends well. Jo-Ria heard her before?"

"No, though Siroth and Ajirth have."

"Those two hissed?" Ziz-ka sounded surprised.

"Bad shift and both were carrying little ones when Molurth approached them unwisely."

Ziz-ka blew out a soft breath, "Those are the biggest females on station and he's the tiniest."

"A very lucky tiniest member of our race. Agata moved like she did now and they forgot Molurth. While her hum doesn't fill the same range, it covers the core. Curiously, our females recognize human females as same gender."

Bron looked up at the two Aqu-jios, then at Agata easing the case towards Jo-Ria with her foot, the top opened now.

Jo-Ria's hissing stopped as she snagged the case then whatever the bartender prepared before moving backwards.

The female security team swept around Jo-Ria as they vanished down another hallway.

Agata rubbed the back of her nape, then spoke to the bartender.

The bartender gave a hooting crackle, before placing a sealed container marked as 'Human-safe food' in English, Spanish, Chinese and Russian along with the six core languages of the space faring Aqu-jio. Agata lowered her whole body, the Aqu-jio display of respect and thanks, before turning to Lorth.

"Lab again tomorrow?" she asked.

Lorth lowered his whole body, mandibles drooping, "Again. Enjoy your food. We both are off-shift."

"You just finished?" Ziz-ka asked as Agata walked away.

"We were already off when we heard we needed to help a hisser," Lorth shook, "Jo-Ria is more frightening than Siroth and Ajirith combined."

"Only when she's forgetful. Maybe we should have the caretakers drop off her food and keep her company until she eats? It worked well for the fourth layer."

Bron focused on Ziz-ka, recognizing the term.

Fourth layer meant a specific military command level internal to the Aqu-jio. One lower than the Low Guard of the Web, those who protected the rulers of the Aqu-jio. Two lower than the High Guard of the Web, who were surpassed only by the rulers of the Aqu-jio who were called collectively, the Nest.

Ziz-ka must have once been a part of the fourth layer to speak so casually about it.

Pondering this unexpected side of her partner, she went to collect their meals as the two chatted about solutions to keep Jo-Ria from another hissing fit.

Chapter 7
Bunker Under the World

"So they brought a plague. Fortunate we prepared for them to operate as we would on an inferior world," the CEO of Patriot Corp, Charles McDonnell twirled a pen, "For something that looks so domesticated and friendly, they are like us."

"They used their looks and demeanor to fool all our operatives on the ground. Even our human lie detector was easily swayed by their lies," the head scientist, Rowan, chuckled, "They must have suppressed their own desires just long enough to take what they want with guileless subterfuge."

"At least we're secured," Charles twisted his chair slightly so he could smirk out over the slave floor, "Plenty of debtors to rebirth our society to the correct form, without those pesky first world countries holding us back from our rightful place."

"Afris and Southcans," Rowan snorted in disgust, "They don't understand the scientific process. A few test subjects dead and they whine about statistics. The end result justifies the process, even if a few perish from unknown circumstances."

"On that train of thought, how is the vaccine for the plague coming?"

"Slow. It isn't anything like what we have records for," Rowan tapped his eyebrow, "They are clever beasts. I will find the cure, though we may lose a few hundred debtors while I experiment."

"We have two million on standby, should you need more subjects," Charles smirked, "I do love a good downturn and desperate people. We get our pick of the brightest who ran afoul of our well timed stock drags, all the first world countries none the wiser about our role in it."

"With a cure to this plague, even the first world will bow to you," Rowan laughed, "And I will have more assistants and minds to clone for my projects."

"Just keep the results rolling, Rowan. You'll get all the brain-power you want."

In the corner, the debtors serving them shivered in horror.

They hadn't wanted to be enslaved, but the market crashed taking their meager savings and their life from them.

They shuddered as the cruel men leading the Patriot Corp discussed the death of every human being on Earth as if it was good business.

Cursing in her head the capricious and toothless government that lied about protecting its people, she curled deeper in the meager shadow, hoping she'd escape their attentions for at least a night.

If she didn't have one night's respite, she didn't want to contemplate her next actions.

She only knew they would be dark and sinister as these ugly powerful individuals striped her humanity away.

Chapter 8
Alone in the Crowd

He grinned as he looked out over the view from the outpost he got assigned to.

The first human-Vish'Tarin combined science expedition in history. The third non-Vish'Tarin joint expedition in the history of Vish'Tarin people.

Beyond the thick glass lay the mostly untouched wilds of Vish'Tarin Forty-Three.

It was hoped with a human along, the Vish'Tarin could begin to thrive on this world.

Or so the Aqu-jio said when they offered him the job.

Smiling, he sighed happily.

He wouldn't have to be around any human for at least a year, maybe more, save for remote medical checks.

The Vish'Tarin scanners made the machines back home positively simplistic in comparison.

It also meant no exhaustion keeping his perfect mask in place to placate an archaic view of masculinity. One that belonged in the caveman era and not for space travelers.

Inhaling, he admired the view he rapidly grew used to.

To be in the center of so many intellectuals and brilliant minds would heal a part of him that lay empty for so long.

Since his mother divorced his father for his abuses and cruelties.

He'd been fortunate he had been in college at the time and not subject to custody battles. His father would have killed him, either mentally or physically if he'd been forced to live with him.

Momentarily captured to the dark past, he wished he knew what his mother did nowadays.

The law prevented him from finding out what she did as it, in turn, blocked her from hearing his exploits. Something about mothers who divorced for any reason lost all right to their children, even if those children needed their mothers more than their fathers.

He'd traced it to a malicious corporation masquerading as a legitimate business.

They knew women fared worse when single or divorced than men. Took advantage of it to enslave them as permanent debtors.

"Stress-signs rising. You collected?"

He turned, smiled, "Sorry. Thinking of wrongs in the past, partner."

The gooey mass spread then contracted, the pico-bots translating for him, "Wrongs not righted?"

"These wrongs cannot be righted. Only borne until they fade," he replied easily.

"Source of wrong defeated by mass."

He took a moment to figure out what his partner, Slysosh, meant since the translation between their two species wasn't perfect as yet.

"This wrong braced by bigger and firmer mass. Not easily washed away nor consumed," he stated, hoping his meaning came across.

"Stress-signs never good. Come mass with us."

Looking one last time out at the wilderness, Daniel grinned, "I think a discussion would sooth my stress-signs to background noise."

Slysosh speedily oozed across the floor, "Solid and flexible mass form stronger."

Carefully moving after his partner, he banished the specter of the law's devious cruelty from his thoughts.

He was a scientist here to collaborate after all. He would do no less than his mother would expect him to.

Besides, he could find out more about the two types of Vish'Tarin: Solid and flexible.

Chapter 9
Kooks and Spiders

Agata locked the door behind her, grateful to have escaped the persistent man wanting her to give in.

As if women only thought of sex with men. How did all the stupid dunces find her desirable?

Sighing, she set her food box on the side of her chair, slumping into its customized form.

Automatically, the chair massaged her tired body, loosening her tensed muscles.

"Continue show," she ordered, pulling her food out so she could refuel.

The voice over was translated from the Aqu-jio speaking on screen, "After several hours, the scout ship managed to sync their image generators to the new alien species, sending through the image of the mission leader, Forithz, issuing the standard greeting."

Agata smiled at the spindly Aqu-jio with yellow-black markings lowering his body in the greeting, mandibles twitching, "We of the scouting team of Star Webs greet new species. May we grow the universal web together."

She snorted at the first glimpse of the human faces, the part alarmed, part confused expressions, whispers she knew by heart echoing in her room.

"What is it doing?"

"Captain, I think it wants to eat us."

"Their ship is six times ours, captain."

She laughed lowly as an hour full of attempts to speak between the two ships ground to frustration.

The Aqu-jio narrator continued, "Initial translations took some time, as evidenced by the lack of comprehension with the species that we'd learned was called humans, or homo sapiens. However, the translation systems worked tirelessly to provide the foundation for two species to work together."

Forithz churred unhappily, "These individuals don't seem to be intelligent enough to understand we are trying to speak to them."

The narrator added, "This is when the second in command, Food Chief Jix-za, offered to make the next attempt. Being a more brawny looking Aqu-jio, she hoped to showcase a different body type."

Jix-za tapped the controls, showing her thicker legs and more muscular body, "I am Second in Command Jix-za of the scouting team of Star Webs. I greet from one intelligent species to another."

The human captain whispered, "We aren't getting anywhere."

"Maybe we should put kook on? She's the spider lady," the second in command suggested, "She can't make this worse."

The captain leaned out of view, stated, "Hydroponics? We got aliens that look like your friends. Open your vid-screen."

A cheerful voice called, "I was just watering the mosses, can't this wait?"

"They could blow us up while you are watering," the captain clicked a button, "They may do that if she's as weird to them as she is to us."

"Fortunately for the Aqu-jio scouting team, they would meet their first peer among the humans," the narrator stated respectfully, "Please note, that at the time humans did not consider the person responsible for their food to be of high rank, unlike most civilized worlds in the Aqu-jio travel web."

The view from the Aqu-jio side filled with a dread-locked haired, black skinned woman, with a tarantula sitting on top of her head.

She beamed out of the screen, "Hello! I'm Doctor Amanya Noman. Greetings from hydroponics," she stepped back and revealed the rows upon rows of plants, vines and tubes, then she gestured up at the tarantula, "This is Howard. He's my best big bug catcher."

Forithz hummed, "That on top looks like us. Are the other ones its servants? It seems to be seated on it."

Jix-za rubbed her mandibles, "They brought on their second. See the food grown behind it? That looks just like many food growing pods across the web," then Jix-za hummed loudly, "I am Second in Command Jix-za of the scouting team of Star Webs. I greet from one intelligent species to another, and fellow food care-taker."

"The tiny rider didn't respond," Forithz tapped his legs.

"Look, the one we took for a chair is attempting to communicate!" Jix-za danced excitedly.

Doctor Amanya was humming and chirring on the screen, the tarantula on her head moving more animatedly until it scurried over to a vine and climbed out of view.

The human captain groaned, "Noman, don't try speaking spider to them."

She replied, "They are acting different. I think they may be trying to communicate."

With a slow gesture, Amanya raised her hands, curving them up and down like a spider's, before tapping on a pipe in a repeating pattern.

Jix-za rubbed her mandibles, "It's trying to speak to us. It must be the sentient species. The tiny one like us didn't stay."

"We have a partial translation," the communication Aqu-jio chirped, "Want me to try it?"

"Go ahead for our side," Forithz ordered.

Amanya paused then frowned, "I think traditional noises of my lovelies isn't right. Trying to speak theirs may be harder since they have a wider vocal range."

Agata choked on her meal at the first translated words from english, "I are trying to speak them. My loves' normal voices not reach, maybe due to lack of sense."

Forithz turned to Jix-za, "More time?"

"The main body of the Star Webs will be within range shortly. I rather make the attempt before our larger webs arrive and scare these ones away."

"Open translation both ways. We'll speak with the second in command."

"Translation running in five seconds. Go ahead."

Jix-za waited then spoke slowly, "I am equal rank to you. My name is Jix-za of the scouting team of Star Webs. The caretaker of our food. What is your name?"

Agata leaned forward at the first Aqu-jio words rang out, ones she memorized since they changed the history of her people, just like the moon-landing and mars-landing did.

The emotionless tone sounded artificial, "I same title. Jinna named of fleeing stars, searcher. Take food care. Name you?"

Amanya squealed, "This is so great! Hello fellow Doctor Jinna of fleeing stars. I tend hydroponics, and the least ranked on the crew. My name is Doctor Amanya Noman."

The translation back flashed in text on the Aqu-jio screen, as it was hummed, "Wonder! Greetings peer second Jox-rath of shooting stars. I am low rank of water plants. Name is second Amina No-person."

Forithz cocked his head, "Low rank? That can't be right."

"Least ranked?" The translation offered back in English, "Not correct."

Amanya scratched her head, "Umm, I am the least ranked on board. Wait!"

"Low ranked, yes. Cling," the translation offered in Aqu-jio.

Amanya pulled over a hover whiteboard, "I'll list our ranks, then you'll understand. I'm here, lowest of the low ranks in hydroponics along with my assistant Jenny," her pen squeaked on the board, "next is maintenance, who care for our ship. We have two of them, Jack and Tina. Then is Engineering, those who make our ship move and fabricate new parts. I'll list only the head of it, Max. Above him is medical division, who Brendan acts as chief of. Sciences is next, followed by communication departments. Then our third in command and second in command. Then our captain. See. I'm lowest ranked."

Jix-za gave a low hiss in outrage, "The caretaker of food should never be lowest ranked. Without food, nothing else would be done."

The translation gained some clarity and an angry tone, "The one making the food is never lowest ranked. No food makes all other positions meaningless."

Amanya beamed, "I've been telling the Space Agency that should be the case for years. So where are you ranked, Doctor Jinna?"

Jix-za calmed her voice, "My name is Jix-za. I am second in command. I tend our version of water plants."

The translation's tone softened, "Correction in translation: My name is Jix-za. I lead as second. I tend our type hydroponics."

"I'm glad your society recognizes the importance of hydroponics, Jix-za. I wish mine was as advanced to do the same."

Jix-za muted the line, "This is wrong. I think the first ones to come on are your rank or mine, Forithz."

"Can you diagram our rankings in a similar manner?" At Jix-za's body bow, Forthiz turned back on the sound, "Jix-za will set up a picture like yours. Would you wait?"

Amanya nodded, "I look forward to it."

Jix-za pushed a hexagon shaped surface into view, explaining the words, "This is our ranking for this ship. Forithz," Jix-za tapped Forithz with a leg, "is leader. I am second in command."

Amanya frowned once Jix-za was done, "You said this is the rankings for your ship. Does that mean you have a fleet?"

"Fleet? What is fleet?" Jix-za asked.

"A group of ships is called a fleet."

Jix-za hummed, "Yes. We are scouts to the Star Webs, Webs is our fleet."

The human captain's horrified whisper broke the moment, "They are scouts to a fleet. Where is their fleet?"

Amanya snorted with an eye roll, "I have a better question, captain," she erased the board, then drew the star system of Alpha Centauri, "My ship is trying to get to this star system. Would you be willing to help us?"

The communication Aqu-jio offered, "That appears to be the star we were going to scout. Maybe theirs?"

Amanya heard the translation that sounded near perfect to Agata, "Oh no. We don't own it, but we want to explore the star system. We'd be the first to step foot outside our star system. Maybe start a colony."

"Noman!" The captain hissed.

Forithz interjected, "I will reach out to our fleet. We would like to help you spread your web. There are some dangerous space faring species and we would not want you to fall prey to them."

"That would be excellent! I think this would be a good time for a rest while we discuss with our respective crews."

Jix-za bobbed, "Yes. Trading food care techniques can wait until later. Also what is with the tiny Aqu-jio like creature you had on your head."

The narrator interjected, "The two ships switched to communications to their respective groups. We will show the Aqu-jio side in this program. The human side will be provided as a link after this program."

"Forithz of scouting ship requests urgent line to both Star Webs highest ranks and to higher ones," Forithz rubbed his mandibles with respect, "We have met a new species. Their food caretaker has requested assistance."

The narrator added, "Due to first contact procedures, the High Guards of the Web are signaled to listen in, so they can report back to our leaders, the Web. You'll see one of the rare times the Web entered the communication strands to weigh in."

"Tah-rix of Star Webs is listening," the gruff voice announced as a wolf spider looking Aqu-jio appeared, "Their food caretaker needs assistance of what form? Do we need to have sciences work on supplements?"

Forithz lowered his body, "They say they want to go to the star system ahead. With the reports of the Zinxirs in the area, I do not think it's wise to let them go unescorted."

Agata inhaled her food wrong, coughed, then gasped, "What?"

The program paused, and the station's voice asked, "Would you like some additional information, Agata?"

Trembling, images of the smirking and amused face haunting her nights filling her vision, she asked, "The program said there were Zinxirs in the area of the star system named Alpha Centauri at the time humans and Aqu-jio first met. Is that true?"

"Per our records, they intended to take over that star system due to its natural resources. It is why the Star Webs were dispatched. Zinxirs tend to take one star system and turn it into hundreds, and this star system was too close to a new trade route to be taken lightly."

Rubbing a hand over the back of her neck, Agata inhaled, then exhaled, "Thank you. Please continue program."

Humanity had been much closer to extinction than she heard about in history. Zinxirs hadn't been met until four years after the first contact with the Aqu-jios.

"Do they know of the Zinxirs?" Tah-rix asked with concern, "If not, what is their technological level?"

"We are currently taking a break since it took some time for the translation to reach a decent stage for communication," Forithz snorted, "They are barely at interstellar travel. I request sciences to review their ship. I have further concerns for their safety."

"An eighty-six percent chance of critical failure?" Tah-rix's mandibles shook in shock once the science crew submitted their report, "How they got this far without dying is beyond comprehension."

"This is Kioxiz, High Guard of Web," a high pitched voice spoke when a frail looking bright orange and green spotted Aqu-jio tapped the edges of a web chair her species preferred, "The Web wishes confirmation of Star Webs' science report. Please send all data and strands forward. We'll have all allied species review as well. While waiting, know there are now six reports of Zinxirs in your immediate vicinity. Two of them note war ships, old style."

"Are there concerns with us offering escort to the new species?" Tah-rix requested, "We are after all going to the same location."

They discussed positives and negatives for a while, then a new voice broke in.

"The Web wishes to speak."

Agata leaned forward, eager to hear the voices of the almost legendary rulers of the Aqu-jio.

"The Web, sector seven is listening," a deep rumbling voice almost growled, three shadowy shapes appearing on the screen, "sector eight and eleven are here with me. We reviewed the scouting reports of the star systems around the one you are going to. The Zinxirs may not be allowed to claim any worlds there. The most advanced world, which our science advisors suspect is the place your new species call Prime, would be annihilated in three hours with one war ship. Two in the area does not bode well for them. We are dispatching two more Webs to your area. One will chase the Zinxir out, while the other makes a nest near the species' star system. No sense in letting these young ones die when we can help. Your orders are to provide all assistance to the ship you've encountered. Especially to the food care taker. That this species prioritizes other positions higher than food is worrisome to all of the Web."

Tah-rix bowed his whole body, "We will begin rendering aid with the scouting ship, then the rest of us once the Star Web catches up.

We'll accelerate slightly to ensure if Zinxirs arrive before their foes, we'll be able to protect the new species."

"The Web concurs with the approach. If your sciences have difficulty, all allied science divisions have been put on alert for assistance. Relay all further information to this strand for dissemination. The Web returns to their strands."

Tah-rix indicated Forithz with a leg, "See what the food caretaker needs first and foremost. See if they have needs besides food."

"We transmitted their rankings along with all recordings. The maintenance and engineering ranks may need supplies as well, since they are so low in rank," Forithz offered, "Request our supplies be checked for materials their ship is made of."

"Star Web caretaker listening," a voice Agata recognized spoke, "We have enough pods of raw materials to remake their ship ten times over."

Ziz-ka appeared, his body younger and more vibrant than she'd ever seen him. Floored she worked with a Aqu-jio who'd been at first contact, she watched with increasing awe.

"Prepare in case they need it. With an eighty-six percent chance of failure, I'm worried they will need all of it to just reach the star system, much less make a new strand in their web on those planets," Tah-rix gave a frustrated sound, "Forthiz, this strand will be monitored at all times in case of emergency."

"Acknowledged," Forithz bowed, then turned his head, "The other ship is reaching out for contact."

"Get the ship's name along with the species name. We'll add them to the tracking systems in case any traders arrive at your location."

Agata slumped back, her mind whirling.

The Aqu-jio actively protected not only the first contact ship, they'd moved to ensure the vicious and manipulative Zinxirs never made a stronghold so close to Earth.

One Zinxir warship, even an older version, could have wiped out humanity before they managed to make contact with the Aqu-jio or any other species.

She'd send out her thanks Doctor Amanya Noman serving on that ship for the rest of her life.

Watching the rest of the program, she listening to the eager Amanya chatting with the shocked maintenance and engineering teams as the scout ship offered raw supplies to ensure their ship continued.

At the end of the show, as the human ship descended in the wake of the scouting ship, the Aqu-jio ship a shield to the frail human one, she smiled at the ease the humans and Aqu-jio melded together their efforts.

She hoped to continue in the same vein with her partner.

Chapter 10
Checklist

Gregory Smithson smiled as he walked back to his quarters.

Down to one woman left on station to bed.

He admitted that getting Bron early on have been to his benefit. Besides Agata, she was the hardest one to get into the mood, according to all the gossipmongers.

His checklist never got so close to completion this early in an assignment.

He may go back through once he checked the box for Agata.

Being friends with the alpha gossipmonger had its benefits.

Agata hadn't had a sexual partner for some time, like several years.

She was due for a celibacy break.

Chuckling in his head, he entered the human section, looking over all the others coming and going.

The highest ranked human on the station, Captain Stefan Garcia, nodded briefly in passing, acknowledging everyone equally.

Gregory hid a smirk. Good ol' Stefan wasn't a normal man.

Good thing, or Gregory wouldn't have gotten a chance at Agata. The Captain's type was Agata in a male version.

It also helped there was slim pickings for men on board, especially when the laboratory crew was recalled to Earth.

That meant all the smart, driven and powerful women on board were his to sow his seed with. Smart women meant smart children.

With the human law preventing the termination of any pregnancy, even when the woman's life is in danger, he'd get a few children out of this group.

Strong children who'd continue to grow his family.

He had sixteen children so far, all with their moms. All becoming fine men.

Since he was blessed with so many male children, he hoped to get a few female children in there.

It was fortunate he'd been born in this era. Earlier ones would have garnished his wages to pay in support of his children, regardless of marriage status.

The women brought the children into being, they got to rear them. Just like his old man use to say.

His old man also said to sow his seeds among the brightest and strongest. It's how Gregory came about after all.

Humming to himself, he entered his quarters, glad the Aqu-jio supplied large ones even to the lowest ranked humans on board their station.

His last jig had no room for getting it on with women.

This station he could use his rooms, her rooms, or the alcove off of the environmental controls for the human section.

He really liked the last one, but Agata wouldn't relax enough down there for any gratification. Being medical she'd be utterly concerned about the location.

Other notes he found on her swirled in his mind.

Her husband had been persistent until Agata gave in and married him.

Gregory couldn't use the same approach, or he'd be too much like her husband. A hard rejection was significantly more difficult to work around than a normal one. He didn't want lingering taint from Agata's husband to keep her from seeing him as a man.

Her schedule wasn't predictable week to week, so he had to bribe the filing division head clerk to get a note on her shifts. Though that sometimes didn't work as she and her Aqu-jio took extra shifts enough it messed with his plans.

He perfected the middle steps for his plan.

Agata had a sweet tooth for green tea and chocolate shakes made by the bartender, especially when packaged with the chili smothered beef burritos.

He just needed the time, which bed and how to approach her remaining to be sorted out.

Gregory grinned as he planned how.

Chapter 11

Vibrating Strands

Agata frowned at the listing freighter as the other medicals on station observed.

Since she and Lorth were acting seconds and had been off-duty when the notification came in, the chiefs of medical set out to see what the medical emergency the freighter signaled help for.

As per standard in medical emergencies with Aqu-jio stations, thirty fighters escorted the medical transport over.

If anything happened, those fighters could either rescue the medical staff on board along with survivors, or contain the issue so it didn't spread further.

The Aqu-jio ships floated to their positions, forming a sphere around the freighter.

"Lorth, are all readings copying over?" The chief's voice rang in Agata's ears clearly.

"Confirmed. Limited signals from inside, or they are partially shielded. If limited, only three of two-hundred crew registering. All those remaining are human."

Agata scowl deepened as she read the data, "Low heart rate and minimal electrical activity registered from the pico bots? How is that possible? Pico bots take in their energy from those they are attached to."

Lorth's mandibles flared, "The electrical signatures are the lowest I've seen. The closest equivalent was a suit on the edge of failure."

"We are moving toward those. If the pico bots energy level were even lower than that situation, it could account for the heart rate reduction and the desperate edge in the communication," Jourth spoke calmly, "Fighters, enmesh the web to third layer."

Agata translated the last to mean the fighters in space to be ready for immediate action.

"What was that?"

Agata leaned closer, squinting at the dim view from the human Chief Medical's suit, "I don't see anything, Doctor Nells."

"Listen," he replied, "dragging steps."

She could hear it faintly, "Possibly. Limping with one dragging foot if human."

Then lights flared to life, burning away the darkness.

Only to reveal horrors.

Aqu-jio desiccated corpses, or pieces of them, flung against the hallway, some halfway into what looked like air ducts, as if trying to escape something.

"I'm Nick," she heard over the line as her vision caught on a human child crouched between two Aqu-jio, as if seeking their protection, "I'm the human Chief of Med Staff on Aqu-Jio Station Kol-zia, who are you?"

The hairs on Agata's nape bristled at the girl's jerky movement, "Doctor Nells, be cautious."

"She's a scared little," was all he got out before blood sprayed and alarms klakoned a human's suit was breached.

"Nick!" She called, as Lorth relayed, "Jourth, your partner is under attack."

Staticky words filled the line, ".... dead... eb.... tain... huma... full... esh... contain!"

Lorth called out the fighters, "Enmesh to burn cocoon!"

Agata shivered as he gave the order to begin escorting the ship to the nearest star and to shoot any evacuees if they tried to leave.

"Agata, inform Command," Lorth turned to the communication channel the medical division, "Third Strand, Medical. We have a full enmesh ordered at Aqu-jio Station Kol-zia for inbound ship."

She turned to the internal channel, "Acting Second of Med Staff to Command."

"Command listening," Captain Stefan's face sternly glanced to the side before focusing on her.

"We have web containment protocol activated. Relay to all parties to proceed," Agata looked back as a horrible gurgle came from Nick's still open line, swallowed.

"Strand will remain open," Stefan's partner ordered, "Link the open lines to us as well."

She tapped the panel, doing that.

Gagging behind her made her whirl.

To feel her entire body recoil as the girl's face appeared on the screen.

The only sounds she made was the chomping of her teeth as she ate a hunk of flesh, the tanned skin inked with a tattoo clear to see.

The same roman inspired image of Apollo Nick bore on his neck.

"She ate him!" One of the juniors panicked.

Agata turned and ordered, "You, get to the labs and inform them we have data loads coming in. Move!"

The junior hesitated before running out.

"You two, inventory all human drugs on station. Now!"

Agata issued orders, getting the horrified humans into action.

Lorth whispered, "You told me cannibals were rare."

She glance at another screen, fought her animalistic need to flee as humans fought over a human security guard sent with the medical team, tearing the woman to pieces.

"They are. Always in time of desperation. What concerns me is our suits shouldn't have let metal and debris through," Agata wrestled her professional persona forward as a wall against the images on screen, "She tore through it as if it wasn't there. How?"

The exterior screens showed remote driven engines dropping from the fighters to grapple to the ship. They switched on, moving the ship in the direction the fighters would take to the star.

The purest form of purification they possessed.

Everything living thing burned in the corona of a star.

"Agata," Lorth tapped her shoulder, "We are now the Chiefs of Medical Staff."

The weight of the responsibility on her shoulders felt like planets on her shoulders.

"What caused this?" She asked in a harsh whisper.

"We'll find out. I hope at least one of the security can subdue your kin."

Chapter 12
Cornered

Jourth quivered behind the security detail, sealing his missing fore leg as fast as he could, restating into the line, "Half of medical are dead. Web containment now. Human partners dead or contaminated. Full enmesh ordered. Confirm order for web containment!"

The human male had attacked from an air duct, landing on the back of a security Aqu-jio ahead of him.

Jourth snatched the back of the suit and attempted to toss the human down the hallway.

Only for the human to turn and gnaw up to the first joint on his leg in an instant.

The security detail managed to get their plasma fangs above the chewing mouth quick enough to free him, then haul him behind their bulk.

Then the scorching webs were shot out as a mob of more crazed humans appeared, more than the three they registered.

He'd retreated to the center of the group, issuing the order to get the ship underway to the nearby star, following plague protocols.

"Jourth, we need to retreat back to medical," one of the security lashed out with his leg tips, searing a human in half.

Only for the human to crawl towards them with a clacking teeth and empty eyes.

Scuttling backwards, his team and him raced away from the parts trying to catch up with them.

"Zombies," one of the security detail hissed, "They really have undead creatures."

Jourth couldn't argue with the evidence before him.

These humans kept chasing them, even if they possessed only one arm or leg available to move forward.

He repeated the call, hoping Lorth heard his command to lock down and scorch the ship clean.

Even if they survived long enough to understand this human illness, they had to keep it from the station.

Cures were not instant things. Long, agony-filled experience spoke to that truth.

He stopped before running into the security member leading back to the medical wing.

Due to his angle, he could see why they halted.

Another human, though this time, they wore frayed remnants of their suit, as if the pico bots had stopped functioning.

The human launched at them, making them scramble backwards, yelling warning to the rear guard.

Only for the human to turn to ash, drifting down while a brilliant flare hurt their eyes, partially blinding them.

"Come now!" An Aqu-jio ordered, one with a new voice.

They ran after the voice, following pass piles of ashes and long dead bodies of their kindred.

Clearing his eyes, Jourth picked out a black shape so tiny he almost mistook it for the spider plushie toy Agata cherished above all other possessions.

One of the tiniest members of the Aqu-jio, the Cranny Granny clan, they could squeeze into spaces most Aqu-jio couldn't.

They also were the most vicious and venomous of all clans, defending their webs with the fierceness of ancient mythic warriors.

A pressurizing hiss of air sounded behind him as the Cranny Granny stopped.

"They can't get in here, yet," the tiny Aqu-jio quivered, "How many humans joined you?"

Jourth answered, "Twenty-seven, including my partner."

"They will be infected soon, if they aren't already. It started in the humans we picked up from Human Third," the Cranny Granny hissed angrily, " then caught all our humans like a swift falling web on prey."

Jourth looked over his group, realized only five security remained and himself, "Does it catch us as well?"

"No, the humans do. They eat us like a female does a male when she's been isolated too long from sustenance."

Shaking from the analogy, he asked, "How did you survive?"

"Air ducts so tiny the humans cannot enter them. My domain as part of the maintenance team," the Cranny Granny pointed to the side, the easily overlook hatch open and barely big enough for the Aqu-jio to fit.

"Did any others survive?" He asked as the security detail scouted the room after patching their wounds with deft manipulations of their suits.

"No. The humans ate them all, leaving husks for those bits they didn't consume."

"What did the humans do after eating all the others?" Jourth would fulfill his duty to get as much information as he could out to the station.

It was the last act he would perform in honor of his home nest.

"They followed me where I went. They somehow hunted me, even deep in the bowls of the ship. I lead them to the food stores, hoping they'd eat their fill there," the Cranny Granny hissed angrily, "They wouldn't eat. Let it spoil. Even fresh didn't tempt them from my path."

"Zombies," the security rumbled unhappily, "Human films say go for the head to kill zombies."

Jourth looked at his tiny group, saddened so few survived to this moment.

He should have taken the request for smaller Aqu-jio to assist. The ceiling climbers would have had the strength to pin a human and let him get samples.

"We need to get this information out to the station," Jourth lowered his body to the Cranny Granny, "I'm sorry, but we are bound for the star."

"At least the star has a merciful ending for us," the Cranny Granny pointed to the hatch, "I can scurry through to a point where the shielding is weaker. If you give me a transmitter with a wire, you may be able to reach outside."

Jourth pulled open his pack, then gave the Cranny Granny a suitable device, "You should connect with it as well. You may have seen, heard or smelled something important in this."

"Two weeks is all it took for it to overcome them. If it will spare even one more of us, I would drift in space until I curled in death. If those things get in here, you'll need to move quickly. This map isn't great since some of us tried to barricade the hallways, but it may get you where you need."

The Cranny Granny vanished into the hatch as the map displayed on his helmet. He sent it to the security detail, "I rather have our route before they get through."

The others circled together to plan while Jourth looked at the door they'd entered through.

Though he couldn't hear it well over the sounds of air and engine, he felt the dread-filled rhythm of pounding through the deck.

Like hundreds of human hands hitting the door.

Chapter 13
Solo End

Had it really been two months?

He shivered deep in the mine, shaking as the horrid digging echoed all around him.

Others like him had gone to ground when the evil fuckers had as well.

The so called "patriots" locked their doors after stocking provisions. He knew why now.

After each of his fellow doomsday preppers went radio silent, starting in the country that once had been the land of the free, his paranoia grew.

Reopening the mine's lowest shaft, the one old reports listed as where the remains of coal miners in the bygone era had coughed their last breath, gave him solace but for a scant day before the echoes reached him from the surface.

The break of wood and iron barring his home from the outside called warning down to him right before his cameras caught sight of them.

The skeletal and gangrene rotted bodies moving silently but for the clack of teeth as they moved quickly.

Each door and barrier stood no chance as they inched closer to his last bastion.

The pit to the coal miners called him, whispers seeming to reach him with comfort as the insanity reached the final wall.

Shaking, he swallowed, holding the old style shotgun with slick palms.

Why hadn't he gone with the girl who thought zombies would one day kill the world?

At the time she'd been wildly off in space, her eyes spinning in their sockets as she practically screamed the zombies were coming.

She'd have been dug deeper, or made a zombie proof room.

He had a rock wall between him and the horde scrambling on the other side.

One he knew wouldn't hold, even as the first zombies scrapped their hands and arms to nubs.

Fresh ones continued to push forward, crushing the front line, or shoving them aside.

"Partner."

He jerked, looked at the mine shaft, his gun pointing down into the abyss.

He knew he heard it. Heard the soft voice with a faint drawl like from the archaic westerns.

"Come on, partner. You don't wanna die up there," the voice crooned.

Looking at the walls, he gulped.

Stones were shaking from the walls, the scrap of bone on stone getting louder.

Shuddering, he stepped to the edge and looked down.

Darkness swallowed the light.

"Ride with me, partner."

Coughing, he didn't smell the putrid stench swelling in his bastion, chasing out the cleaner air.

He stepped off the edge.

Falling, he looked back.

To find falling bodies tumbling after him. He swore one had the same twirling eyes of the zombie prepper.

Then he struck ground, bones snapping as he howled in pain.

Only for the undead to crush him into silence, the twirling eyes zombie's teeth the last he viewed as it chomped down on his face.

Chapter 14

Communication Strands

"Fourth strand listening," the calm voice spoke softly.

"We received reports of humans attacking Aqu-jio and fellow species at Human Thirty-six and Human Fifty-one. Both have undergone lockdown procedures. In addition, a ship approaching our blended station with humans has ordered the immediate containment and star cleanse of a freighter. Request wisdom."

"Two human worlds and a freighter cleanse, hmm," a warm voice echoed in the strands, "What are the details on the freighter? What species were onboard?"

"Aqui-jio and human only for sentient, master of Fourth Strand. In addition, there are cows from earth as non-sentient along with two containers of tarantulas spiders, as per the manifests."

The scrawny Aqu-jio, on the cusp of demotion to training up the next generation, rubbed his mandibles slowly, before ordering, "All humans and areas with humans are to be locked down immediately. Web containment to the entire Aqu-jio travel web."

"Reasoning, master of Fourth Strand?"

"The same feeling as before the Zinxirs set a trap for us at Aqu-Jio Two Thousand and seven. Better to pull the web and then release it than to not pull it and have our webbing pulled down from under us. Prepare supply drops for species impacted along with military response."

"I need more than feeling to justify destroying fellow sentients on ships traversing my sector in accordance with the web containment procedures. What pattern do you see, master of Fourth Strand?" A pure logic Aqui-jio stated calmly.

"Those two human planets are practically on opposite sides of the human web's outer strands. The station is outside those webs by one month travel. Whatever is causing humans to attack has spread across their web as fire following the silky strands. Or that is what the pattern looks like. If the High Guard of Web listening disagrees, I will gladly step down early."

A slow threatening hiss made most listening lower their bodies, "Io'lix, High Guard of Web, agrees with additional information. A third human world, Human Third, has sent a message requesting medical and science help. All hailing calls are not answered."

"Begin cocooning all human and human touched worlds. Assume this started at least three months ago, to account for travel times within the human web," the master of Fourth Strand issued the command, "This strand will be open to all emergency communications and coordination."

All those on the strand began issuing the orders, their militaristic speed triggering responses as the web began to isolate humans and those who'd been near humans, the science strands being alerted along with medical.

"Additional order: identify highest ranked human medical or science officers. We may need their wisdom," the master of Fourth Strand watched the display turn from glowing white strands to black as the fastest sectors complied with orders, "Along with any military commanders we can use to keep the peace among their kin."

"Assuming they have not succumbed to this madness?" The logical Aqu-jio questioned.

"Those in isolated spots may be our most useful allies. Many had to travel for years to get to their positions. Seek those first to build their strand and communication lines."

Bending to the task, he began his duties to ensure the web containment was followed to the extracting pattern they'd detailed out to all species who joined the web.

"Human Prime military strand is silent," the High Guard of the Web hissed, "as is its medical and science strands."

Pausing in their work, the nervous rubbing of mandibles filled the strand.

"Then who is the closest in ranking we can speak with?" Master of Fourth Strand asked, knowing someone had an answer.

"Highest rank confirmed in communication is Captain Stefan Garcia on the station that turned away the freighter, followed by Lieutenant commander Bronislava Julija at the same nesting. All other higher ranks are silent in their strands or communication strands are broken," the logical Aqu-jio turned grim, "Both are available for orders as confirmed in our treaty."

"Have them issue immediate lockdown using human terms. All humans to go to their webs and stay there until confirmation of health. It is best the secondary systems to supply nourishment are activated and remove waste material are brought online."

A pause preceded, "Captain Stefan, Lieutenant commander Bronislava and Chief of Med Staff Agata Morales are confirmed as contained in command and medical pods respectively. Incoming medical strand priority report from freighter. Confirmation of infection as human borne...with Aqu-jio as carriers."

The hush made the strand almost tremble when an arctic voice stated, "The entire Web is listening."

Chapter 15
Clearing the Webs

Jourth hissed angrily at the medical device as it reported a failure on his proposed anti-gen.

The humans had managed to breach their previous location, so they fought their way to the med bays.

Jourth tripped the vacuum protocol, sealing off medical from the ship, and in doing so revealed the "zombies" decompressed like regular humans when exposed to space.

The Cranny Granny stayed at the edge of the ship's shielding, rather than join them, saying it had enough of humans. Plus the sun would welcome it first.

Finding no fault with the logic, they spoke little as the time until they met their fate waned. With communication with the station restored, Jourth collaborated with Lorth and Agata as they were now co-Chiefs of Medical Staff.

Agata took the order to isolate rather well, considering the information he'd related.

She'd insisted zombies didn't really exist, not like the human shows. The security detail countered with a rather impressive list of documentaries from Earth, including one about evil residents.

Her scathing reply still rang in his mind, "Humans loved scaring the living daylights out of each other. It's why all those movies are listed as fiction! What's more scary than a horde of undead zombies coming after you? Do you think the sentient bugs that mimic people are real, too? No! It is fantasy. Imagination! Humans have great and terrible imaginations."

"What of the ants and the fungi that make them zombies?" The Aqu-jio argued.

"Check for the fungus. Here's its coding," the display of the scan appeared on all their screens, "If it's responsible, a simple fungicide will eradicate it."

They'd worked on the cure for several hours as Agata used the isolation computer to run lab scans, process results and return failed solutions.

They eliminated fungi and bacterial sources and their treatments.

Progressing on the viral paths thus far turned up no answers.

It had no known similar pattern from the human databases.

Agata started the slog through the Aqu-jio databases in conjunction with the lab staff on station.

Jourth set aside the medical device in frustration, slumping to the floor in exhaustion.

"Eat," the human movie Aqu-jio offered a tube, "You have been running three times your norm."

"I've done quadruple shifts during an emergency and not felt this bad," Jourth took the tube then let his mandibles hold the tube so he could slurp as he tapped his legs on the floor.

"Lost of your limb?" He offered.

Jourth sent him a look, stated, "I've lost six while a medical, ten while in the military. Not a shock anymore than the hideous rehabilitation for such wounds."

"The humans turning into zombies?"

Jourth swallowed the tube contents and crumpled it, setting it aside, "While an odd enemy to face in our final hours, not as bad as facing those who betrayed us then mockingly butchered us."

Picking up the medical device, he ran it over himself.

Cursed.

Opening the line to the station, he relayed, "Lorth, add Aqu-jio can carry the same pathogen as what the humans have."

"We received the same information from the military strands a brief time ago," Lorth grumbled, "We are scanning the humans for signs every thirty minutes, Aqu-jio and the other species every hour."

"Look at the scan I sent. If an Aqu-jio has brittle carapace syndrome, they will be slightly impacted," Jourth wanted to curse.

Lorth made a contemplative noise with his mandibles, "I see it now. It looks like it is causing the pico bots to redirect to fighting the infection rather than dealing with the symptoms of brittle carapace syndrome. We'll have pico bots introduced to handle the brittle carapace separate from normal infection groupings. Assuming any others have the same situation."

"Are the pico bots helping to contain the pathogen?"

"Partially. Not good enough to keep the Aqu-jio from joining the humans in web containment," Lorth relayed.

Jourth tapped his legs in rhythm, staring out at the still remaining zombies.

"We'll try to restrain one of the humans and see if we can clear the web of desiccated remains."

"They may kill us all before we can do that," the security detail began moving, resetting their weapons.

Jourth looked out, "I can't assist you out there. Go with my hopes."

The security detail crouched, preparing to leap as Jourth triggered the vacuum seal to begin re-pressurization.

Chapter 16

Sulking with a View

Daniel buried the rage at finding out right as he was going to step outside for the first time he was to return to his quarters and stay there.

Indefinitely.

He'd been under house arrest for four days.

He couldn't even join his hosts during meal times, or converse in person.

It was all over digital devices and distance.

He was supposed to go out there and help his partner with thriving in this land.

Instead he was grounded to his room like his mother did once upon a time.

Blowing out an aggrieved sigh, he slumped into the chair next to the window to enjoy the view while he could.

By what Slysosh stated, all humans and Aqu-jio were under containment, supplies being arranged from those stored in automated depots. Drones would deliver their cargo, then become scrap for use since they wouldn't be returned.

Admiring the efficiency and caution in the design of such systems, he scowled at the landscape beyond.

"Daniel?"

"Slysosh? Good news?" He leapt up and went to the door, looking down at the image of his partner hopefully.

"I bring dreadful news, and a neutral one," Slysosh quivered unhappily before hurriedly speaking, "Drone scans of most human worlds show no living masses."

Daniel fought back a flicker of panic, forcing his logic to lead his questions, "There are masses?"

64

"The masses...the groups of humans they record are moving dead. The Aqu-jio marked them as zombies."

His head spun, "Zombies?"

"Yes. Humans infected eat their kind and others. Several human transports have been found drifting with true dead, or so filled with zombies, they've been escorted to stars for purging. The human leader masses are gone."

"Who leads then?"

"Military leadership is held by Captain Stefan Garcia, massed with his second Lieutenant Commander Bronslavia Julija on station near star Polaris."

"What of sciences? Medical? Food?"

"We have enough supplies to keep you fed long pass your lifetime, Daniel. Sciences is currently under Doctor Karmal Landris, who is at the laboratory planet Jorid. She is there with sixteen other human scientists. Medical for our sector is handled by Doctor Agata Morales."

Swallowing in fear of the barbed law that kept his mother from him, as well as him from her, he asked, "I need confirmation of Doctor Morales family lines and work partner."

"Important?"

"Under human law, yes," he detested the law which made him a prisoner long past when he'd served jail time for just overhearing a co-worker detailing his mother had been posted on a space station with her long time partner Lorth.

Slysosh's color darkened in waves as he communicated over the pico bots to others in his mass, then lightening again.

Fractal-like patterns that oddly soothed, he noted numbly.

"The records mark seal on family line. Partner is open: Lorth of mass called Cometspinners from Aqu-jio Prime."

Rubbing his face, the harsh promises the prison guards echoing in his mind, "Human law prevents me from knowing my mother's whereabouts and any interaction with her. If this is her, I can't see her, nor her me."

"Prevent massing? Your leadership mass gone or missing."

"It's the law!" He gasped at his bitter voiced replied, "I'm sorry. I have to follow the law."

He turned and fled into the bathroom.

His mother could be the medical for his sector and he couldn't see her.

Cursing the demented and cruel denizens who'd formed such a barbaric law, he leaned against the sink, fighting back tears.

Horror of what Slysosh said filled his mind.

The worlds of Earth were filled with zombies.

Real world zombies that shouldn't be real at all.

If only monsters didn't exist, he'd be free now.

Only they marched, one from his kind and one from the dead.

He really needed a hug.

With the promise the future dreams could be made reality, rather than an empty husk crumbling away.

"Mom," he whispered without hope.

Chapter 17

Burning Clear

Agata rubbed her eyes, the headache threatening to tear her skull in two.

The medical isolation chamber was built with little comfort in mind.

Plus the screen wasn't prepared for a determined human rushing to get answers.

Between all the science divisions working on curing the "zombie" plague across the galaxy, no match above seven percent had been found in all the cataloged diseases, viruses, bacterium, fungi and other pathogens.

"Agata, it's time."

She stood and looked out at her weary partner, "I'm not sure of the procedures for a star purifying a ship carrying our predecessors."

"Silence so we can listen to their final wisdoms," he lowered his head, laid it on the thick glass tiredly, "Then we observe a minute for each life lost on the ship from our station."

"An hour," she murmured, closing her eyes in grief, "I wish I could do more to help, Lorth."

"We are doing all we can, with what we have," he reassured softly.

Tears threatened to overwhelm her voice, "Lorth, out of hundreds of billions of human lives, we are down to less than ten thousand. They are scattered throughout the stations and planets, waiting for diagnosis, either to their death or a fractured life. Those who were on ships like the one we are watching the death of have either joined with star coronas, or are screaming to be allowed to live. What more can we do?"

"These procedures and protocols work, but they tear the web we've formed together," he spoke gently, "We'll live and reform the web into a new pattern, perhaps one which stays. We will be strong together."

She straightened, nodded as her shoulders weighed down with the horror of so many of her kin dead by a plague which shouldn't exist.

Along with the burden of knowing the Aqu-jio who'd freed her from an ignoble demise all for divorcing her ex, was about to met his end in fire.

All because of a zombie plague.

Zombies weren't real.

Until now.

Moving to the screen, she tapped it over to the exterior feed of the doomed freighter.

"Jourth, we stand on the edge of the web to feel your wisdom in our legs," Lorth intoned over the communication line, his formality conveying dignity and respect.

"I appreciate that," Jourth appeared sitting on the floor, his body shaking terribly from the brittle carapace condition the pico bots should have been addressing, but for the zombie infection, "We'll listen from the youngest to the oldest."

The smallest security Aqu-jio spoked softly, "Charge your spare packs and be ready for combat. Even the most fragile species can be deadly to the strongest. Let my wisdom vibrate through the web."

Agata fought back tears, as the second Aqu-jio paused, then broke into some side to side shuffle, hops and leg taps.

"Dance, even if it's the last thing you do. Let my wisdom vibrate through the web."

Agata let the tears fall as they got to the last of the security.

"Enjoy other species' entertainment, even the most fantastical," the Aqu-jio gave a sad hum, "As there are grains of truth in them that lead to greater understanding. Oh, and human zombies are real."

Agata swallowed the laugh wanting to rise from her. She wouldn't dishonor them in their final moments.

Then the security Aqu-jio helped Jourth to standing, though his legs couldn't hold him anymore. Flakes drifted off his suit, signs the pico bots were just excavating the dead cells, rather than recycling them.

"All it takes is one strand weakening under an onslaught to tear the whole web. Each new species we ask to join us strengthens us just as it weakens us in other ways. Be strong for each other and cocoon those weaknesses we can," he looked out of the screen, "To those humans who tremble on the part of the web still whole, look to the future you wish your kin to take. Even at your lowest, we will help you."

Agata sank to her knees, hugging herself as he finished, "To the Aqu-jio who listen across the strands of our mighty web, the humans brought something we lacked. Imagination and fantasy. Even if they wish such stories hadn't become real, their strength comes from their rich and wonderful minds. Those who are clear of this plague need our strength to reform their tiny webs so they may support us once more, even if it takes centuries. Let my wisdom vibrate through the web."

All those on the ship hummed, "To the Web we give our lives."

Then a strange voice called out, "I offer my wisdom as one who started this journey with many, and leave it alone. Let this wisdom echo through all strands. May those small be clever in seeking safety in hidden crevices, those who guard stand firm against threats inside the web and beyond it, and to those who lead, screen all ships better so this is the last which touches us all. Let my wisdom vibrate through the web."

Jourth huffed then they all repeated, including the strange voice, "To the Web we give our lives."

Agata watched the screen vanish back to the exterior view, polarized so sensitive eyes could watch.

The ship shuddered as its military escorts pulled back.

Pieces peeled off, instantly scorching as the metal began glowing.

It felt like a long time as the metal slowly burned brighter, deforming as the star compromised the shields and ship systems trying to fight for survival.

Then it exploded, the pieces seared into oblivion.

Shuddering with silent sobs, Agata grieved for those brave individuals who fought to the end, and to the many who'd lost their lives to this horrible plague.

Long past her tears had dried on her cheeks, Lorth broke the awful silence, intoning for the record the deaths of their colleagues, time and cause.

Then he tapped the glass, "Agata, take some time to rest. I'll have the bartender send your food up when you wake."

Her voice felt like rusty knives in her throat, "What of us who live?"

"We find the cure and ensure it never rises again."

Wiping her face, she crawled into the medical berth and let exhaustion claim her chaotic thoughts.

Chapter 18

Bound to Monsters

He growled, struggling against the bindings holding him in place.

Patriot Corp sold his contract to these monsters, all for a fake cure-all.

That's what the bitch-faced aliens laughed about as they bought buyers into what they called the birth floor.

Kyle screamed into the gag as a slimy creature touched him, squeezing his stomach before feeling up his prostate.

"This one for my next child. He has the right waste to feed it to its birth. You have good selection. Secure?"

"We are glad you like our inventory. With the Aqu-jio focused on the awful plague, they won't miss a few humans. Nor would they try to check over their rights. Not this far outside their web, anyway. We can guarantee your child will be born without medical interference."

He blacked out while the slimy creature implanted an impossibly huge egg into him.

When he came to, it was to sharp claws digging into his jaw.

The face smirking at him looked so much like his favorite labrador, he wanted to puke.

"You will last a long while. Many children will exit you to their bright futures," it let its tongue hang out, "pity you require so many special nutrients. It will be years before you pay half your contract."

Screaming through the gag, he raged at the dog alien, promising pain and punishment.

"You males break so easily. The females are strong, having borne your pitiful baby like tantrums. They'll leave their contracts far sooner than you. Of course, they can bear twice as many children as you quibbling brats."

The pat on his head was full of condescension as he strained against his bindings.

Just as the egg wriggled deeper into him, sending agony through his body.

Parasites.

All of them were vermin that deserved demons torturing them for ages.

He'd last.

He'd beat them, even if he had to stay tied there for years.

A flicker in the corner drew his gaze.

A spider web, delicately balanced across two beams waved in the light, before more buyers entered the room, bearing more foul pains for those unable to fight back.

Chapter 19
Orders and Laws

Bron filed reports, read new ones, wrote others, relayed commands from the Aqu-jio military command, then took a moment to process all the news threatening to drag her down into depression.

So few humans remained, almost entirely cut off from one another.

It had been a week since the destruction of the freighter, and the news kept growing more dire.

Bron was lucky in that Stefan shared the command level isolation chamber. She had human contact.

Agata was alone in medical, while the rest of the humans resided in the human section of the station.

Should they be determined to be clean of the plague, they would be allowed to roam again.

Until then, the bartender sent up meals and supplies.

Bron reviewed the videos contained in the drone reports from Human Prime, from Earth.

Cities abandoned to consuming fires or floods as technology failed in the absence of humans.

Shambling hordes roamed the wilds, crossing deserts and mountains to find any remaining humans.

A large cluster gathered at a mountain range once called the Rockies. The images showed them digging with their hands until they had nubs left.

Maybe it meant some humans sequestered deep underground, or something else drew the zombies there, distracting them from humans struggling to live.

Or she let hope linger rather than end it peacefully.

A hand covered her shoulder.

She looked up at Stefan.

"We have a request to impose a martial injunction for a solo human."

Frowning, Bron asked, "What human law is harming us?"

Ziz-ka's voice filled her ears, "A divorce law, which is separating mother from child when that mother is the chief medical for the sector."

Bron stood from her chair to gather with Stefan at the glass separating her from her partner, "I need more details."

"According to the law, whoever divorces first loses all access to children, even adult ones. Familial connections are put under seal, any information gained, even if overheard accidentally leads to immediate arrest, regardless of intent."

"That one was rejected by my homeland," Bron sneered, "We had enough broken families from our civil war, we weren't going to make it worse by adopting the corruption from the oligarchy controlled third-world country. I would rather strip that from our law books."

Stefan asked, "Who is involved?"

"Solo human among the Vish'Tarin, Daniel Morales indicated there may be a possible breech of this law involving Chief of Med Staff Agata Morales."

"We need to confirm via the records," Stefan held up a hand to Bron, "I know this is an archaic hold out from the past, but we need to proceed cautiously. We've already lost more than we can ever recover from in our life time."

Bron snarled, "I won't let such anchors overheat our engines and set us adrift."

Stefan grumbled, "We are military. When this crisis ends, and it will end," at her glare, he snapped, paused then exhaled, "the politicians and lawmakers will take over. They may need this to enforce families staying together."

"This is a horrible law and doesn't need to sully our culture or people one more second."

Ziz-ka huffed, "Do I need the human scientific leader to weigh in since I can't ask Agata?"

"Yes," Bron stated to Stefan's, "No."

"Bring Doctor Karmal Landris on the strand," Ziz-ka ordered, "At least to break this stalemate."

"Karmal online," the deep voice spoke with warmth, "What scientific item needs my attention?"

Ziz-ka explained as Bron and Stefan faced off.

"We have the data from the second Dark Ages in this area pre-law and post-law. The analysis shows it causes more suffering, less family cohesion and here's the nasty part of it straight from the history books: It was crafted to force women and men to suffer needlessly when they escape a marriage that is dominated by abuse and manipulation. I vote to have it stripped from our laws and consigned to history where it belongs with a note on who brought this sadistic, non-scientific piece of garbage into being."

Bron blinked, "Which lawmaker?"

"Lobbyist, for the company called Citizens First. You'd know it better by its fourth rebranded nomenclature: Patriot Corp. The history around it is the CEO at the time was about to lose three quarters of his fortune as per the law of the time until he bought off enough lawmakers. They made true his wish to leave both his wives without their due fortunes because he couldn't stick with one wife," Karmal leaned back in her chair, "History should lead us to better outcomes if we listen. This supports my vote to pick off this tick since we can't support blood-suckers with our population in dire straits."

Ziz-ka offered, "If it makes you all feel better, the Aqu-jio can use the clauses in the treaty to override this. Being as web containment protocol is operating right now."

"No," Stefan shook his head, "Humans will decide this. We have two No's to one Yes, with one vote invalidated due to ethics. Motion to remove divorce law has passed."

Ziz-ka questioned, "Invalidated due to ethics?"

Stefan nodded, "Agata cannot give her vote, one way or another, which leads to invalidation. Human custom."

Ziz-ka gave a curious hum, "With the law now removed, should I have Lorth deliver the news to Agata?"

"I'll relay to Agata as Captain," Stefan inclined his head to Bron, "If you would take Daniel?"

"On it," she stated, moving over to the view screen and began the communication.

After she relayed the change to an obviously confused Daniel Morales, she sent him the official paperwork via interstellar communication.

"Military Fourth Strand has issued new orders in agreement with medical and science," the leader of the station called, "Humans at the following locations are deemed clear of the plague based on projections of plaque spread and timing."

Bron breathed out a breath at the station being listed as clear, "I can get a shower and sleep in my own bed."

Stefan rubbed his neck, "I'll need an hour at least before my next shift."

Ziz-ka replied, "Take the time you need. It has been many days since you were forced into there. A rest may give us answers."

Bron left as quickly as her legs could carry her.

Sleep in her own room sounded divine after staying in the isolation chamber.

Chapter 20
Pushing Too Far

Gregory collected his meal from the bartender in person, glad to be free of the human section.

It also meant he saw his next bed partner entering from the medical section, looking exhausted and hungry.

Smiling he sidled up to her, "Hey, Agata."

"I have no interest," she stated sharply, giving her order to the bartender in a far kinder voice, "Go after someone else."

"We could blow off steam from being under lock down," he purred in invitation, "Plus we start making more babies so humanity doesn't end here. I bet you would be a great mother."

She looked at him with disgust, "No interest. Bug someone else."

He placed a hand on her wrist, stilling her motion, "I want you."

Snatching her hand back, she growled, "Leave me alone. I don't want a lover nor casual fling."

"I'm here if you want, or need me," he smiled charmingly before sauntering out with his meal.

She hadn't taken the bait.

Shrugging, he figured her attitude was because of the isolation rather than her not liking people.

Maybe in a day or two she'd settle back into a routine.

Once she was back to normal, he'd try again, maybe add a little stimulant to goose her libido if she turned out to be celibate. All it took was an unguarded drink to encourage more friendly discussions.

Agata took her meal and rushed out, using her brisk pace to carry herself out into the station proper.

Turning to a table with his fellow men and women, he grinned.

Her tone was angrier, but that was just a facade. He'd release her from it.

After all, he may be one of the few last men in the universe she'd have access to. He was better than all the rest, so he'd win in time.

Chapter 21
Check-up

Agata inhaled, exhaled.

Nerves jittered through her still as she triggered the long distance system that would enable her to be on a distant world for a physical check-up.

Her pico bots synced with a container on the Vish'Tarin world set aside for such needs.

It was an odd feeling of an amorphous mass rising from a container before her normal senses took over.

Looking at her hands, she flexed her fingers, feeling the pressure of fingers against skin before she relaxed.

"Greetings, medical mass."

Agata looked to the side at a ooze clinging the wall at eye height, "Good day."

"That phrase translates funny."

She curtsied her body, "It is an alternative greeting humans use. Hello, good morning, good day, greetings, salutations, and many more all reach the same purpose of polite meeting of two or more sentient beings."

The ooze quivered, "You speak as the Aqu-jio do."

"My partner is Lorth of Cometspinners via Aqu-jio Prime. Humans are very quick to adapt to new situations when in the company of wonderful partners."

"You mass well with those outside your mass?" At her polite hum, the ooze seeped off the wall to race across the floor, "Come. Partner to scouting mass is inside protection."

Her stomach twisted into knots as she followed at a sedate pace, moving gently after the Vish-Tarin.

Even with the assurance from Captain Garcia, she was hesitant to cross the line the laws laid down so long ago.

However, her duty as Chief of Medical Staff for this sector meant she had to fulfill it, in spite of the human bindings.

The glass pane looked identical to the one she'd familiarized herself during her isolation in the medical section.

She hated it, since it sealed her off from her partner and friend.

"Fellow mass arrived," the Vish-Tarin called, "Mass together for better health as two instead of one."

"To a stronger web," Agata replied easily before shifting her gaze into the room beyond.

For her heart to lurch with recognition and love.

Daniel swallowed, "Hey, mom."

"Mom? What does this mean?" The ooze asked, colors swirling in a clear sign it spoke with others of its kind, much like the coral-like species Agata loved to give physicals to. They liked listening to humming while being examined, sharing what they saw and heard with their peers.

"I bore Daniel inside until he could be laid, hatch, then grow on his own," she stated softly, using the Aqu-jio equivalents, "I helped him by ensuring food and nurturing him in my nest until he could go to his own web."

Daniel coughed, "Slysosh, she means I split from her as a tiny mass, then while I grew to full size, she chased off those masses who would consume me, allowing me to eat nutrients by myself."

Pride swelled in her heart at how he spoke equally with the Vish-Tarin, Slysosh.

"Mass name?" Slysosh asked her.

"Agata of Morales via Human Prime, if we use Aqu-jio way of naming. To humans, I am Agata Morales."

Daniel sniffed back tears, fighting a smile.

"To humans, Daniel is my son, as I am his mother. We share a last name, though that is not always the case for all mothers and children."

Agata knew she delayed the next step, even as she helped the Vish-Tarin to understand her species.

Daniel swallowed, "Want to come on in, mom?"

"I'll transition to the pico bots in your rooms," she spoke gently, before she mentally asked for the transfer.

As she collapsed, the image of a melting witch crossed her mind.

How ironic she mirrored the wicked witch after being doused with water.

Then she rose on the other side of the glass, taking a few seconds to settle into the new set of pico bots.

A pain lanced through her mind, before it eased.

Doing this took its toll since she was commanding the body over an interstellar communications rather than a planetary version. If he was merely on the other side of a planet, even the largest habitable one, she'd have no issue, nor a head ache after she disconnected.

"Would you like privacy?" She asked, the normal questions coming to her easily.

Unlike her motherly side, which cringed at her professional and formal tone.

He scratched his head, looked at Slysosh, "I think it's best they can see us without the cover of clothes. They still think my clothing is a sentient protective shell."

Agata smiled, "Technically we have three protective shells: our suits made by pico bots, our clothes, and then our skin. Of course two would be classified as sentient in that they are tied to us."

His chuckle warmed his eyes.

With the ebbing of tension, she proceeded with the examination, using the pico bots in her borrowed body to take samples, record data and confirm Daniel's health.

Using the pico bots briefly to run all the necessary tests on site, she opened her eyes, "According to the summarized results, you need more hydration and sleep. A slight reduction in vitamin A would also be recommended, so I'll supply diet recommendations for alternatives to those vitamin A heavy dishes so you can select them twice a week for replacement. Please review your exercise activities in light of your restrictions. I do not know when you'll be able to be released, or under what conditions."

He sighed as he shrugged back on his shirt, then slumped unto a chair, "This was easier before the plague. Are we sure it's not rats again?"

Agata shook her head, settling into another chair, "I wish it was rats, or fungi, or a virus we could instantly cure, but it's not. We have to take time to find a cure."

"It wouldn't be so bad if I could explore out there. I came here to help my partner to tackle this world and behold its wonders," Daniel pouted.

Agata could see he needed a vent session, something she and him both once scheduled for weekends when her ex wasn't around to spoil it.

"I know it's difficult to be held back from your goals. Sometimes the rest of humanity makes choices that end up costing us our dreams, or merely delay them. Have you thought of what you can do to help the time pass?"

"I use to game with a group that spanned all human worlds. When I go into the channels, it's just silence. They all are gone. Playing alone was okay before, but now..."

When he didn't continue she sighed, "When you know there's a whole universe of your kind out there, you don't feel lonely, but to realize you may be one of few left sucks out the hope to find a friend when you need it most."

Daniel scuffed his foot on the floor, "I miss this."

Agata nodded, "As have I."

"How do you handle it, when you are the medical leader?"

Agata shook her head, "I work, focusing my mind. Then I go back to my bed and all the burdens heap on my shoulders. Then I get up and work again. Because doing the job is sometimes all you can do."

"But I can't go out there," he stood stalked to the window, setting his knuckles on the glass, "I so want to be out there, so at least I'm doing my job."

"The best I can do is give you a hug through these pico bots," she offered.

"I," he froze looked at her, "pico bots. I use to play a game where you had to go to a room set up for running around on a moving floor. Do you remember it?"

"Yes. Dexterous Dexter. You loved the feeling of running through hallways, climbing mountains, flying through canyons, then coming out to only need to take the elevator up to our floor. Why do you ask?"

"Is it in the Aqu-jio systems?"

"Why important?" Slysosh requested from the glass.

Agata nodded to Daniel, indicating she wanted to know as well.

"You are here, even if your real body is on the station light years away. If the pico bots here can be modified to act as a virtual reality suit for me, I can maybe use the Dexterous Dextor program to give the pico bots a cohesion and abilities. If it works for me, we can use them with the Vish-Tarin to send out scouts that can be damaged without hurting us."

Agata sorted through Daniel's excited speech and shrugged, "I'm no programer. However, they would need to reduce the pain and pressure responses so it's more a glove than a duplicate. If you went out with the same system I'm using, you'd experience the agony of the pico bots if they are harmed, just like if its you out there."

Slysosh chimed in, "We know masses that can help. They make drones. If example of this entertainment is available, we can mirror."

Agata bowed her head, "I'll send a request to the Aqu-jio archive and see if they can send the records over to you both. Then you can work on a solution."

Daniel bounded over, hugged her, "Thanks, mom."

She embraced him, knowing she wasn't really there, but still enough to help him, "If you need company, there are some Aqu-jio who play human games. If you are alright with the idea, I can send you the link to the group."

"I'm not lonely, mom," he countered, but half-heartedly.

"As your partner would say, mass with like minded masses. When the loneliness comes, you are with others," she smiled, "I may not be able to come to you every time you need me, so hopefully they can offer a bastion of safety."

She stood, then kissed his fore head, "I will do my best to find a cure."

"If anyone can, it would be you. You'll come when you can?"

"At the least, I will be here for your quarterly physical, and," she gripped his shoulders, "If you get sick, I doubt my beef enchilada soup recipe has made it out this far. I'm sure I can make it with this double."

"I really miss your churros. Dad never let me get our recipe box."

"I'll have it sent to you with the other links. A few would help with your alternative meals."

He kissed her cheek, "Thanks, mom. I can see if I can get my dream back on track," he looked at Slysosh, "And get out there with my partner."

Slysosh glowed, "Yes, mass for scouting. We will find way with our new mass."

"I have to get going, Daniel. See you later."

"Bye, mom. I'm glad they got rid of the awful law."

She stepped over to the container, then replied, "So am I."

Dissolving back into the container, she picked up the pico bot group outside the glass, before being escorted back to where she began.

Slysosh commented, "You split off a strong mass. See where his mass gained strength in solitude."

"I am grateful he has a strong and willing mass to join him on exploring this world. I know I will hear good news from you in the near future."

"Yes. You go mass for others in need. They will be able to survive better with your mass nurturing them."

"We all need to mass together. This plague is a nasty mass that has infected us all."

"Truth. However, we have many masses working toward same goal. Also, Aqu-jio supplying food and materials from their vast stores is space. Mass will not die out."

Agata nodded, "That is my hope as well. Thank you, Slysosh, for guiding me to my son so we could mass."

Like a click, the words cleared up, "He needed you and you came. Your strength is greater than we expected. Many races leave their children to fend for themselves."

"Some races have children that need care to grow into strong adults. If the law of humanity had been different, we both wouldn't be where we are now."

She stepped into the container, curtsied to Slysosh.

"If that law wasn't there, where would you be?"

Sadly, she answered him, "On Earth and most likely dead. Until he needs me again."

She dissolved down, then blinked her eyes open.

To wince and close them again.

Lances dug into her mind from her eyes, a sure sign she'd been in the link too long.

Then blessed relief ran over her mind, "How is he?"

"He has a direction to move, plus some adjustments to help, Lorth," she smiled, "I got to hear a change in the translation between human and Vish-Tarin. Daniel's doing a great job on that front."

Peeking up at Lorth when the silence stretched uncomfortably, "Has something happened?"

"Most of those who are not human refuse to enter medical unless those who are human are not present."

Agata swallowed her reaction, "Am I confined to quarters?"

"I would think that is wise. If you are willing, a secondary review of the computers analysis is underway. It's looking to confirm the computer correctly eliminated possible sources of this zombie plague."

Tedious and monotonous work, however, one she'd take.

Being a medic meant she had to put those coming in for help first, her damaged and wounded sense of self second.

"I'll be in my quarters then. Normal contacts?"

"I've let them know you will work on this while I'm handling non-humans. If a human wants a kindred touch, I'll let you or the other human medics know."

She nodded, then walked out.

Bigotry had no place in this day and age.

If only they could change such attitudes as easily as the savage and heartless law which kept her from her son, until now.

Chapter 22
Breach of Civility

She hated them.

She wanted them all dead.

They caused this. They caused the economy to crash, they broke bank accounts and then broke spirits.

She wasn't a plaything.

Her mind twisted in möbius strips of thought.

If only they hadn't invited the slime ball dog aliens, humanity wouldn't be down to those in the reinforced bunker. Those hunkered down for the end of the world.

Except it was the end inside for those less than the "kings and queens". Like her.

A waitress slave for the main table.

If only they hadn't made her a plaything.

If only they had left the economy untouched.

Destroyers of innocence.

They would do this to the remaining humans once they surfaced.

Claimed the world for men and their consorts.

She hated them.

The tray clattered on the counter, the air thick and heavy in her throat, choking her.

She couldn't breath.

Clawing her neck, she tried to loosen the noose around her neck, her vision narrowing.

Then eyes filled her view, pushing away the grayness.

Electric blue eyes.

They held her still as hands warmed her cold fingers.

A promise lay in those depths.

"We need to get more ingredients for the seven course," a voice echoed down the tunnel in her ears, before she was moving, pulled along with stumbling steps.

The soft click of a door closing jolted her.

She stood in the storeroom.

The tall, beautiful woman before her looked on her with sympathy.

Her eyes filled with the same miseries and hardships.

A sad smile proceeded those blue eyes looking to the side.

When she followed the gaze, she felt as if the world finally righted.

The box she knew well, having purchased and used its contents so often to deal with vermin.

Locking her glowing green gaze with electric blue, she nodded.

It was fitting those who poisoned the world with their greed would die in the same way.

All they needed was time, which those so called kings had bought for them by burrowing so deep into the earth.

Their deal made with no words, the two specters of death swept out, their ghostly vestments hidden from all but their sister in arms.

Chapter 23
Growing Unease

Bron sat at her usual table, noting the tension from the non-humans seemed to only ramp up at her settling down.

Only two humans were in the social hexagon: Agata who looked worn and two decades older than the last time, and herself.

Bron opened her meal, took the first bite, savoring it as she watched.

Not all the non-humans reacted with fear to the humans.

Some of the Aqu-jio and the bartender continued to be cordial, greeting Agata with sympathy and soft words of encouragement to persevere.

Agata nodded weakly, eating her food mechanically. Obviously her mind resided elsewhere, as she didn't pay mind to her surroundings.

Which is why Bron winced once the maintenance man entered, stalking towards where Agata sat alone.

Ziz-ka spoke gently, "I have to give him points for persistence, but isn't there a limit to a human female's patience?"

Bron swallowed, cleared her throat softly, "I've come to the opinion human men only think with their genitalia. With our population so devastated, those like him will push too far and..."

Agata's bellow silenced all conversation, "I said no! I decline! I will not fuck you even if you are the last man in the universe. Leave me alone!"

The last word hit a pitch that threatened to shatter eardrums.

Bron frowned as the man continued to smile and slid closer to Agata.

Then he was hopping backwards, cupping his knee, Agata storming out with her food container, swear words trailing in her wake that would make any dock worker thumbs up in appreciation.

"Was that the equivalent of hissing?" Ziz-ka murmured as the man hobbled out, a smirk on his face, "He seems pleased by Agata's reaction."

Bron rubbed her forehead, "Hissing is the last straw before a female attacks with the intent to devour among your people. Human women are less predictable when they hit that point. Though that high note definitely sounds like Agata's close to that ceiling."

"At least she took her food," Ziz-ka gestured subtly with his mandibles, "Many here would be less pleased if she left it."

Bron agreed as tension increased its pressure in the social hexagon, almost to the point where they'd have to release it one way or a much nastier way.

"I imagine she'd be worse than me if she skipped a meal at this point."

Ziz-ka gave a concerned hum, "Like when you missed two meals and punched a wall hard enough to break three of your fingers, or when you had the migraine and nearly killed the officer who thought sharing his music over the entire station communication strands was funny?"

She looked up, "Latter, or worse than that."

"Hmm. I don't think I want to see such, what did you call it?"

"Hangry. Angry hunger."

"I think the females of my kind would easily adopt the term."

"Considering the remnants of the human race, the term may be all that remains of us in short order," Bron took another bite, then recalled a topic for her partner, "Why was the word for downward progression chosen for your move to this position?"

Ziz-ka chuckled, "Ah. When an Aqu-jio is promoted, it is to teach them how to be better through adversity. The higher the promotion, the more challenges and breadth of experiences you can obtain. If you have obtained enough, you are demoted back to help others being promoted. This ensures the learning we get is passed on earlier for those who are following us. We have less broken lines of learning."

"So you rose all the way to High Guard of the Web before being sent to a teaching position?" Bron asked, resisting the urge to smack him for using demotion yet again.

"No, I didn't need the trials of that level to be qualified for demotion. My web stayed invisible in the sunlight without such experiences. Those who rise to the guards of the web, either low or high, tend to be mandible to mandible fighters so why they can promote to that level. My training follows another path."

Bron leveled a glare at her partner, piecing together their conversations, "Like those who wait for unsuspecting prey then lunge out of hiding?"

"Yes, I did do that. I still have it, since you didn't see nor hear me in the archive earlier. Why were you in the archive, assuming you are willing to share?"

Bron finished her meal, set aside the box and utensils, "I was hoping my view of the patterns in the plague's spread would lead to a faster cure. It looks like one of the games that survived the Second Dark Age, where the player is trying to exterminate humanity by evolving various harmless pathogens into fatal ones before humanity cures it."

"Your people have such fascinating views on morbid topics. With zombies being real, must we be prepared for vampires? I liked the one which separates into half and floats after its prey. The image of its inner organs stretching like a cable is both abhorrent and intriguing."

Sighing, Bron replied, "I just hope vampires stay as myths. I've had my fill of supernatural and evil creatures to last my great-grand-children their lifetime."

"You have children?"

"Not yet."

Ziz-ka tapped all his legs in excitement, "Who would be your partner?"

She opened her mouth to utter the standard phrase of, "Mr. Right," when she remembered the words of the Hir-zt who'd found her after speaking with Agata.

"You humans are far too limited," the words echoed in her mind, "We could outright abolish this wasteful use of female resources. You weaken yourselves so much you never recover. We have almost two thousand alternatives should your species evolve out of its horrendous self-destructive and malignant ways. Two men could have a child, just like two women. We could even do multiple parents to address those hereditary diseases that end a child before they can draw breath."

Bron thought on that, then looked at Ziz-ka, "There's only one human I'd want a child with since they have always treated me with respect and dignity."

"Who?" Ziz-ka leaned closer.

Bron noticed most of the non-humans were paying attention to their tables, so she stated calmly, and a small prankster smile, "Agata, of course."

Chapter 24

Pieces

Agata rubbed her eyes, looking blearily at the clock.

Blinked at the day it showed her.

How had she lost three months?

Sitting up, she frowned at the date, and the side note she was off-duty for two more days.

Like it would do her any good.

The asshole pursuing her would find her and harass her.

Or poison her.

She found out quickly he dropped a significant dose of a nasty narcotic into several of her drinks.

Symptoms included increased libido, mood swings and suicidal thoughts along with withdrawal collection of ills.

It was popular in the third world countries for entangling brides and grooms from the first world countries in matrimony.

Gregory couldn't have known her body had been influenced by it once before, and if she ingested another dose would quickly regress into its dark miasma, most likely without the support needed to get back to herself.

The laws also stated she couldn't report him for dosing her drinks, even if it ended up with her sick, or more likely dead.

Sighing, she stepped out of her bed, dressed in the suit appropriate attire, then made sure her suit covered her.

Then she entered her living room and queued up her show from last she watched it.

"The Aqu-jio met the humans for the first time outside their respective spaceships. Note some viewers may be disgusted by the graphic nature of the historical record."

Agata frowned, then called out, "Station?"

The show paused, "Yes?"

"Why would this show display the historical record rather than a recreation?" in their history shows, Earth lessened the horrible death of two crew members who hadn't checked their equipment well enough for that first face to mandible meeting.

"I do not understand."

Agata rubbed her head, "For humans, we modify the news so it doesn't gross, horrify or otherwise dismay the viewers. Like helium poisoning that is coming up in this show."

"That would be an exaggeration of the truth. Of those species in the web, or have been encountered on its fringes, there are four who use less than truth."

"Who?"

"Inside the web, there are only two remaining: Vish-tarin and humans. A third, the Yuik:Yhu was wiped out by unknown causes a century ago. Outside it is the Zinxirs. Zinxirs are noted for using partial truths or exaggerated truths to convince non-Zinxirs to give up vital resources for pittances."

So a bunch of truth tellers with a few liars or truth stretchers to make it interesting.

"Is this why I'm asked if there really are dragons, elves and other beings?" Agata muttered.

"Are these not real beings from your historical records?"

Agata rubbed her face, sick and tired of correcting non-humans, "With the exception of these zombies, nothing else human has produced in regards to supernatural should be treated as factual."

"I'll append the notes we used for the Yuik:Yhu and Vish-Tarin fictional accounts to all human records. You may be asked to clarify on a case by case basis in light of the zombie plague originating from Earth."

"That one is the exception, not the rule," Agata blew out a breath, "Proceed with the show, please."

She watched the live, real death of the two crew members, the medical members of both ships desperate attempts to save their lives hitting her hard. She knew what those humans clustered around their dead companions felt, knew what horrible thoughts were going through their heads.

Could I have saved them if I checked their equipment?

We should have stayed inside where they wouldn't have died.

Why were they gone?

Why was humanity on the cusp of destruction so many times?

She touched her nape and the scar there.

A physical reminder not to let placid outward appearances to fool her again.

"Pause show," she ordered with a strained voice.

Shaking, she looked back again on the incident, trying to figure out how she almost ended up dead, why she'd been chosen for the Zinxir's traditions.

Lorth had carried a heavy-set Aqu-jio with six broken legs into surgery, leaving her alone in the medical suite.

"What be you?"

She turned, looked up at the nearly seven foot tall alien leaning against the doorway. She found many aspects of the alien to mirror a pet from her homeworld, enough to make her feel less defensive than normal.

Automatically, she curtsied then replied, "I am Medical Officer Agata of Morales via Human Prime. May I ask what you wish to be called?"

The warm brown eyes seemed to soften, "Human? Heard of you from happy traders."

"I am glad my species is well received in the web," she offered the standard polite reply.

Its muzzle wrinkled a moment, as if the alien suppressed a smile, "Using Aqu-jio introductions, I am Lix of Breaker via Zinxir Prime."

Not realizing anything was wrong, she respectfully asked, "Would I be of assistance, Lix of Breaker via Zinxir Prime, or would you like to wait for the Aqu-jio on duty?"

Lix's tongue lapped up around his nose, much like a dog's, "A physical exam can be covered by you, yes?"

"I am licensed up to the third level of regular physicals. If the physical you require is more exotic, Lorth would be able to serve you better."

The happy expression on Lix's face set her at ease, "Nothing exotic. I do prefer privacy."

Nodding her head to the hallway opposite where Lorth worked, she offered, "We have several privacy screened rooms that way."

Lix grinned, flashing sharp teeth, "I will follow you."

Her knowledge of alien species hadn't been nearly as thorough as she believed. If she knew then, what she did now, she'd have known Zinxirs preferred their prey to proceed them. It kept prey from escaping them, either because escape routes were blocked, or they locked their mouth on the nape and thrashed their prey to death.

She didn't recall what happened after she entered the room, only the walk to the door as Lix's body towered over her.

What she recalled next terrified her even to this day.

She woke suspended in a fluid tank, the recognizable tubes coming to her mind easily.

She'd noted each one with detached interest.

Nutrient feed. Life fluid circulation. Monitoring lines, at least six of them. Electrical devices which thrummed noisily in the tank.

Then her side vision caught on a reflective surface.

Her body didn't even jerk as her mind screamed.

What was left of her nape drifted in ribbons around her, her severed spine easy to see.

She should be dead.

That wound should have outright sent her to her makers.

The rest of her body floated below, connected by ragged strands to the front of her neck.

She knew her jugular veins were either gone entirely, or the remaining pieces hid out of her sight.

Fear flooded her mind as she tried to understand what her chances of survival were.

"Agata?"

She focused her vision at a distorted image that looked like a demonic shadow in front of her, the shape blurred against the walls of the fluid tank.

"Agata, I need to you think a clear thought," the voice sounded like Lorth's, "Even if it's what you ate for breakfast."

The statement grounded her, even as the hysteria tumbled through her like a pack of wolves on the prowl.

"I had the bartender's dinner special for humans: Beef vegetable soup with oyster crackers paired with a wine from Human Six. Dessert was mangos mixed in strawberry jello," she tried to say, even though her mouth didn't move.

"I am able to hear you clearly. You know where you are?"

If she could have swallowed she would have, "One of the fluid tanks in medical."

"Good. You were attacked by a Zinxir, a particularly vicious species whom is normally escorted on stations like this. The one who attacked you slipped past our safe-guards and made his way to medical. He waited until you were alone to approach you."

Agata stammered, "Did I...did I cause him to attack me?"

Images of her ex-husband flitted across her mind, his so-reasonable voice as he sneered at her weaknesses and fallacies making her feel frail once more.

"No. You did nothing," he lingered on the word before continuing, "wrong. This species view others in one of two groups: Deal carefully with, or abuse until they can be eaten. They normally default to the latter of the two with newer species, like yours."

"I was alone. Vulnerable," she whispered, mentally shivering from what he would say next.

"If I had known their ship docked, I would have insisted you come with me and called up the back-up pair to staff medical. This is on me, since Aqu-jio are treated in the former group I mentioned. I made the mistake," he hesitated, seemed to change his mind before speaking softly about her injuries, including to her stomach which she could see, "The surgeries for these type of wounds are extensive and agonizing. As you have listed no medical attorney nor a medical decision designee, I need to get your approval to proceed with treatment."

She could rattle off the various steps in the lengthy, bordering on torturous, recovery strategy.

They'd have to knit her body and neck back into one by directing the pico bots at almost the individual level.

Eighty percent of those who underwent the treatment gave up midway and choose the easy death rather than face the pain for one more second.

Those who survived usually suffered from ghost body symptoms, where the head didn't think the body was still there.

The pico bots could keep her heart and lungs going should her head suddenly stop sending automatic signals, but it would require a programming team to go step by step through her whole body to catalog the paths and then get them applied to the pico bots.

As far as she was aware, only three humans successfully survived to physical therapy, which was considered slightly easier than what came before it.

Lorth asked her to decide to suffer and bear the agony ahead to an unlikely recovery, or if she wanted to rest in peace knowing her body was supported by the various tubes in the fluid tank until she eased into death.

"How long until the decision must be made?"

His grim response made her tense, "Right now."

"Live," she said simply though she wanted to cry, "though I reserve the right to cry, bitch and moan about it."

Lorth laid a leg tip on the tank, her eyes seeing the details on his suit as it pressed against the glass, "You'll have to be conscious and without pain-killers for this."

She would have drawn a shaky breath, but she couldn't, "I understand. I hope you'll forgive any screams."

Agata shook as she pulled free of the memories, knowing she'd screamed for what felt like forever. Mental screams couldn't be silenced since there was no throat to roughen into hoarse whispers or worse.

If Lorth hadn't come back when he did, she'd have died then and there.

Just like humanity right now.

Without the Aqu-jio, humanity would be dead.

Clenching her eyes tightly shut, she breathed.

Unfortunately, any human with psychotherapy training or experience had been wiped out with the plague. The plague overtook the conference most human medicals used for networking and learning sessions, and those who remained behind were too close to Earth to escape the zombies.

She didn't have anyone to speak with about her traumas.

But she knew she had less of them because of the unwavering support of Lorth and Jourth. When she thought she'd shatter like metal dipped in liquid nitrogen, they'd bandaged her, body and mind.

Cocooned her until she could emerge from the nest.

Stronger and smarter. More informed about the dangers out in the universe.

Except Jourth died and Lorth led the medical suite without her.

Standing, she walked to the shelf holding her most precious items.

Picking up the plush spider, she cuddled it.

Her son had a much rougher looking version of it when he left home for higher education.

His first toy.

Sometimes she wandered down the happier memory lanes until she got out of her funk.

She hoped this time, walking those memories would shake off the horrors tied to the Zinxirs.

Chapter 25
Profit Margins

They sat around the round table, each one with easy view of the others.

Even among their kind they could be attacked and devoured, hence the table configuration.

Rox licked his chops as he was called to report.

"Our sales exceed expectations. All those species with reproduction methods the Aqu-jio outlawed for humans are spending immense amounts of money to use our merchandise. All for the cost of a cure the humans never got to use."

Muzzles parted as teeth flashed, mocking huffs echoing in the room.

Jav, who sat opposite Rox leaned forward, "Your stock is clear of the plague?"

"We not only ensure all those wishing to purchase use of our merchandise have no scent of the plague as carriers, we run hourly checks for it. Nothing yet," he panted with amusement, "In addition, the Aqu-jio have stopped the spread as anticipated."

"Did you intend for the Aqu-jio to be carriers of the plague?" Jav cocked his head, "That seems convenient in hindsight."

"A happy bonus, I assure you. With them trapped by their own laws, we are free to capture critical targets without their ships coming to intervene."

Jav howled with delight, "We can finally take the systems those humans claimed when they had no right."

"Give it time. The zombies will need to starve to death before we can move in and claim the world," Rox cautioned, "These creatures proved deadly, even to us. A surprising development considering humans are generally weaker and less protected than us."

"You are certain we'll gain those profits?" The oldest member challenged, his greying muzzle crossed with scars, "The expenditures so far greatly exceed our normal boundaries."

"Here are our profits from the humans, minus the upkeep to prevent their early expiration," Rox bristled his nape fur in subtle challenge, "We are already ahead, so your fangless arguments are disregard-able."

The oldster flashed fangs, "I've survived by being far more cautious of my enemies. I can see the Aqu-jio discovering not only the source of the plague, but tie it to others."

Rox clacked his teeth derisively, "You worry too much. You've allowed your eventual death to dull your aggressive nature."

The oldster wrinkled his muzzle in warning, "And the young run swiftly to their demise, gleefully howling their presence to all predators."

"What of these humans in isolated areas," the largest of their kind asked, "With their continual existence, we may be unable to claim their worlds." "The majority of those who remain are men," Rox licked his nose, "Humans adhere to strict taboos against reproduction with the same gender. With less than a thousand women remaining, their species is functionally extinct. We just wait for them to die out. No more than a hundred years based on our projections."

"There is a station full of them in the middle of the Aqu-jio space," the oldster pointed out, "They have access to all the reproductive methods. According to our last remaining spy among the Aqu-jio, two of the leaders for the humans are female. They could simply ask for those methods to be brought online for them."

"Their historical records show they loath non-traditional births. They will do anything, including kill their own to ensure the women birth the next generation as their species have done since they crawled out of the muck. Mired in those limited views, humanity will die out."

The oldster shook his head as if tearing the meat from the argument, "According to the spy's information, two of the three human leaders are women, which is the reverse of the norm for them. Looking at their historical records for women led societies, they take non-standard paths from those led by men. These two could override the man and order humanity supported by the Aqu-jio allies."

Barring his teeth, Rox laughed contentiously, "Women of their kind are frail things. One birth greatly deprecates their mental acuity. The Medical leader has given birth once, so she'll rebel against any new paths."

The oldster stood, "Don't listen to your peril."

He vanished, teleporting to his ship.

The rest mocked the retreat with jibs.

Rox wanted to know where the oldster's ship was so he could teleport onboard and slay the fool.

He'd done enough damage to their kind by surrendering to the Aqu-jio five centuries ago.

If he hadn't betrayed the honor of their kind, the Zinxirs would have dominated the universe, feasting on all the other species until full.

Dismissing the nearly dead fool, Rox joined in on the next discussion, regarding the next species to fall to their dominion.

Chapter 26
Tired Eyes

Agata pulled up the next data set to check over as compared to the plague.

Three samples of the plague displayed on the screen, their structure practically burned into her memory at this point.

"Set completed," the lab leader intoned, "Collecting next set."

She left the lab communication strand open so she could relay her findings and confirm when sets were closed out.

So far none of her sets reached even one percent match to the plague.

Looking at the collection dates listed on the samples, she resisted sighing.

Her current set was from three centuries ago.

She was equally irritated and amazed the Aqu-jio kept samples from diseases for so long.

The human samples barely lasted four decades if they were lucky.

Marking the current sample in the set as confirmed non-match, she rubbed her temples, closing her eyes for a moment. The next sample would load up while she pondered.

Thinking on one of the stories which lasted through the Second Dark Age, she wondered if she may be the experienced scientist studying butterflies who missed the wing colors differed between two species of butterflies. However, where would a young scientist come from with fresh eyes to spot such a difference?

Shaking her flight of fancy away, she opened her eyes.

The match on screen was nearly one percent, elements shared between the two easy for her eyes to pick up.

On her personal tablet she listed the sample reference id, just in case maybe a cure could be pieced together from various sources to solve the zombie plague.

She may be desperate enough to propose such an outlandish solution if all these samples ended up marked as containing no commonalities.

Agata clicked confirm, continuing her slog through the sets, one by one.

At the end of her shift, she'd cleared four sets as compared to the Aqu-jio lab techs' average of twenty.

"Set completed. I am taking a rest period," she told the team.

With their confirmation, she closed the communication line. Stretching, popping stiff joints, she stared at the ceiling.

There must be a cure, or a collection of cures to the plague.

If this real disease lurked among humanity, someone should possess a resistance or anti-bodies against it.

Yet, nothing in human records showed so much as a wisp of this plague. No anti-bodies with unexplained enemies, no genetic component keeping a human from changing into a zombie once infected, nor a folk tale of how to ward off the evil dead.

The Aqu-jio even tried the cures or vulnerabilities for the other supernatural creatures in human records, hoping maybe humanity simply conflated a cure for a vampire or werewolf with that needed to defeat a zombie.

The piecemeal cure may find purchase if they could form a framework.

Looking at her tablet, she picked it up, pulling up the references she collected so far.

Ignoring her body's cries for sleep, she highlighted the sections of the known plagues which overlapped the zombie one, fiddling with the displays to fade the unimportant bits so she could manipulate the image.

Dragging and rotating the similarities, she paced back and for, slotting in the various samples to match the zombie plague.

Time sped by as she continued down her list.

She reached the final one, rotating it nearly a hundred ninety degrees when her mind latched on to what she saw as she hovered over where the sample would slot in.

It fit perfectly in line with four samples near it.

Like someone spliced the samples together.

She set the sample into place, then looked at the spots she identified previously.

She jumped as a buzz sounded.

Her next shift.

Changing her tablet back to the list, she shook off the pattern for now.

She needed to step away from it and think.

By doing mind-numbing tedium instead.

Sighing she opened the line to the lab, picked up the next set, and began to work through it.

Halfway through the set, she stared at yet another less than one percent match and felt her stomach twist.

With shaking hands, she pulled the reference id to her tablet, then did the manipulation of the sample against her current results.

It slotted in.

As if the zombie plague was crafted.

No. It couldn't be. Who would create a plague to kill off humanity?

Unbidden, the image of Lix leaning on the doorway crossed her mind, her heart racing, sweat dripping down her spine before her suit automatically absorbed it.

She dug into the details of the samples she'd identified already.

The samples looked off. Like they too were crafted. Not a natural phenomenon growing from organisms battling each other.

She jolted at her name being called.

"Chief of Medical Staff Agata. I see you haven't taken your first two meal periods today," the lab Aqu-jio sounded put out, "You should take a rest period and address this immediately."

Agata bowed her head in shame, noting she hadn't even gotten through one sample set yet, "Acknowledged. I will address. Pausing on set."

Leaving her quarters, carrying her tablet, she tried to shake off her impression from the piecemeal samples she built so far. In spite of the chill creeping down her spine.

Stepping into the social hexagon, she stopped at the bartender.

A hand circled her wrist, yanked her sideways.

She whirled on who grabbed her, barring her teeth as she recognized the asshole who'd been attempting to poison her.

"Hey, sexy. I haven't seen you in days. You should come sit with us."

In an instant, the barely leashed rage in her broke its chains, goaded by the sick fear in her stomach.

She reared back and hissed with all the air in her lungs.

Chapter 27

Human Calm

Bron stepped into the social hexagon ahead of a security team.

Just as a hiss sounded.

Leaping to the side to clear the doorway, she looked over at the source.

Only to try to scan for the Aqu-jio since she only saw the bartender and Casanova Gregory.

The security team rushed pass her to haul Gregory backwards into the midst of the male contingent.

Bron gaped as she finally saw the person hissing.

Agata's fiery gaze locked on Gregory, her shoulders thrown back as her voice mimicked the Aqu-jio hissing.

The female security members began their dance, but Bron could tell they were tense, the oddity of a human making the noise throwing their plan off.

The hum vibrated the air as they tried to distract Agata.

Bron looked over at the frozen bartender, seeing a half prepared meal for an Aqu-jio held in limbo as the eye stalks stared at Agata.

Agata moved forward, towards where the male security team retreated with Gregory, their nervous mandibles moving in blurs as they scooted backwards.

The whole situation caused a laugh to bubble up her throat, but her professionalism halted it before she uttered it.

Agata stepped forward again, the female circle shuffling to keep around her, their back legs tapping the floor nervously as they varied their hums and dances.

Bron marched over to the bartender, recalling Agata's favorite sweet, one Agata ordered as a reward for her hard work.

"Make a green tea and chocolate shake, large," Bron ordered, then glanced at Gregory who stood confused in the middle of the male Aqu-jio, "Get him out of here. I prefer he was taken to the brig, but his quarters would suffice."

The male Aqu-jio seized Gregory and raced out with him yelping at the sudden movement.

Bron turned back the bartender who slid three full shakes down to stop right beside Agata.

Bron projected her voice, "Agata, drink the shakes."

Agata's gaze finally shifted from where Gregory last stood.

Bron recognized the anger, sympathized with it.

Gregory was an asshole and should have backed off when Agata kicked him.

The fear shimmering beneath the anger made her consider Agata seriously.

Her face was thinner, almost pinched while the bloodshot whites practically yelled of sleepless nights or long staring sessions at screens, possibly both.

The suit sat tighter to Agata's frame than last time, the pico bots compressing the suit to match Agata's lost weight. Skipped meals. Which meant Agata definitely qualified for a hunger-induced outburst.

If no fear shone in her eyes, Bron would assume she was simply hungry and tired, with the addition of being overworked.

"Bartender, two meals to go for humans. Make one a triple portion for Agata," Bron forced her will into her eyes, "Agata, shakes, now."

Agata's hisses stopped, the anger submerging under the fear.

She picked up one of the shakes, chugging the contents as if dehydrated.

"Bartender, add two large bottles of water, and two of apple cider," Bron noted many patrons of the social hexagon leaning away from Agata, whispers of their unease audible now.

"It's the plague. I knew the humans here carried it."

Bron wanted to set the record straight, but Agata's volatility would only worsen the judgements being made if she remained.

"Security, let me through," Bron ordered as she moved towards Agata started on a second shake.

Sliding between them, Bron stood before Agata, letting the Aqu-jio close ranks again.

One of them murmured softly, "What should we do?"

Bron waited as Agata started on the third and final shake, "Clear a path to...the archive. It's the closest isolated spot."

"Do we need to order all human males out of sight," another asked.

"Probably best. Once we are there, I'll get her settled."

"Would she eat one of us? Her hiss sounded like one of us when we are hungry."

Bron resisted rolling her eyes as Agata set the empty shake down, "I'll find out what happened. I may need a runner in case she needs more food or drink."

"We'll stay with you," the biggest female stopped dancing and humming, "Are there calming techniques for human females?"

"Agata?" Bron cocked her head at the haunted eyes that rose to meet hers, "Let's go have a meal."

"Of...course," Agata's voice contained tinges of horror and fear.

Reaching out, Bron hefted the large meal box the bartender slid down to them, "Get the bottles and follow me."

Meekly, Agata collected the bottles, clutching them to her chest as if they were shields, along with her tablet.

Bron walked towards the corridor leading to the archive.

It so happened to be opposite the direction the male Aqu-jio hustled Gregory.

The walk to the archive was done in silence, Agata's harsh breathing slowly leveling out.

Their escort split apart at the door to the archives as if they always did this for humans.

"Agata, would you go in and set up at the table?" Bron requested.

When Agata obeyed, head down and shoulders hunched as if expecting a blow, Bron tapped the door closed.

"I am saying this since I suspect you already contacted Lorth: Agata most likely skipped two or more meals and normal sleep periods. I recommend one of you find out what's she's been doing and relay that to Captain Garcia while I get her calmed down."

"Captain Garcia shouldn't go near her until she's fed," the smallest one insisted, "She may eat his arm."

Bron shook her head in absolute disbelief, "She won't. I'll be disregarding any communications unless they are in person."

Stepping inside, Bron shut the door behind her.

Agata braced her head on her hands, elbows on the table.

Bron set the box on the table, sat down next to her, "What is eating at you?"

Agata shook her head.

"Talk. It makes things easier," Bron opened the box, slid the larger meal over to Agata.

"I have to be wrong."

"About what?" Bron opened her meal, picked up the utensils to take a bite, "Take a bite of this meal. You know the bartender would be upset if you didn't eat."

Agata shoveled in a bite, chewed, "I've been...working on sample cross checks."

"I'm not familiar with that. Can you explain to a layman?"

"The Aqu-jio tried to identify the plague by comparing to every known disease, fungi, virus, etc. None got above the five percent threshold, so we are doing a manual check to ensure the computer didn't miss something."

Bron nodded at the very reasonable process, "How are you wrong?"

"I had a thought to make a cure by identifying all the one percent matches and, well, making a creation worthy of Dr. Frankenstein to address it."

"How is that wrong?"

Agata shoved another bite into her mouth, swallowed, "It wasn't my intention that is wrong. It's what I found."

Agata slide the tablet over to Bron, "These are the samples I started to build into my cure."

Bron took a bite of her meal, broke the seal on the apple ciders before handing one to Agata.

Then she picked up the tablet, scanning the whole diagram.

Immediately, she picked up on a pattern that made little sense to her.

Playing with the fade settings on each matching sample, Bron mentally built the same picture Agata had on her tablet.

"The samples look to have been grafted together already. Almost surgical in its precision on these two matching areas," Bron looked at Agata, "What is the thought you are avoiding, Agata?"

"Someone made this plague. They created it from those samples, but not just that," Agata took the tablet, put the image on the display, "Look at each of these samples."

Bron saw it immediately, "These samples all show a similar pattern, as if they grew in the same environment."

"They didn't," Agata's misery filled voice broke with emotion, "These are from different planets and species."

Chapter 28
Silent

Ziz-ka clicked his mandibles before he entered the archive, having tracked down his partner since she missed her usual punctual arrival at the command meeting by fifteen minutes.

The security detail's story about Agata concerned him enough to enter warily.

He could spare a leg or two. Bron couldn't if Agata attacked her.

Stealthily, he moved so he could see the table at the center of the archive, his eyes taking in the scene.

Agata's shaking hands worried him until the words of their conversation caught his attention.

Bron asked, "Can you bring up the map and show me what you mean?"

Agata managed to bring up a simple representation of the universe, marking star systems to pulse with red color, "These are the places the samples were taken. The first world was overcome with a virus that killed off two of the three genders the O'lirks depended on for reproduction. They died out a century later. The second species died when their ecology collapsed from a fungal outbreak which consumed their food sources. The third fell to a bacteria resisting the drugs which should have taken it down. The species lost three quarters of their worlds to it, pulling back to their sixteenth world until a solar flare scorched them into extinction."

"Do fungi, viruses and bacteria normally have the same pattern?" Bron asked.

"No. Not even in the same environment. These, all of these are crafted, or...they look to be created."

Bron rotated the map, pausing on a view from above the plane of the galaxy, "Hmm."

"I have to be wrong," Agata insisted, her voice roughening, "I can't be..."

"If we put in Xox-xex Prime," Bron added it, "and these four other worlds where civilizations were found destroyed, there is a pattern."

Agata frowned, "Does the Yuik:Yhu Prime fit?"

Bron added Yuik:Yhu Prime to the pulsing red.

Ziz-ka felt a chill run down his legs.

He'd seen the same three lines only once before.

On the battle field, where it was joined by two others.

He spoke, "Add in these worlds," he listed them off as he walked over to the table.

Bron bent to it as Agata hung her head, a display of abject shame he'd seen from Bron only once.

When she'd made a mistake costing the lives of two fellow crew members.

As the new worlds pulsed, Ziz-ka knew without the two humans, the pattern wouldn't have been found.

He brought up the worlds listed on the map, reading the dates of destruction or when the samples were taken.

Spanning almost five hundred years of history, he saw how careful the web had been spun to keep it from sight for so long.

He sent out a signal to bring all the command staff to the archive immediately.

Ziz-ka settled on the other side of Agata, ensuring she had allies flanking her, "Finish your meals. You struck the web just right to warn us where it hung."

Agata looked up, "What do you mean?"

Looking at her and her wan manner he clarified, "You found something of great import. An attack with a familiar pattern."

He tapped the communication strands, going directly to the military channel he knew needed to listen in as the steps of those he summoned grew closer.

"Ziz-ka requests urgent line to Fourth Strand ranks and to higher ones," he spoke as he added the map and the underlying data to the communication.

"Ziz-ka, what is going on?" The station commander asked as he stepped to the opposite side of the table, Captain Garcia looking concerned as he spotted Agata.

"Fourth strand listening," the voice filled the room as images began to appear as the Fourth Strand switch to active status, "Explain why three lines shown in communication mirror part of Zinxir's battle patterns."

Ziz-ka saw Agata eat at Bron's gesture, so he relayed, "Chief of Medical Staff Agata has discovered a pattern from her study of the zombie plague. What you are seeing are the various samples that overlay the zombie plague," he sent over Agata's earlier image, "When the locations those samples came from were appended with those worlds where the civilization had been wiped out without a trace, then the view of the galaxy rotated to what you see, this is how it looks."

The station commander's mandible shook in surprise, "How did we miss this?"

Ziz-ka gravely replied, "Look at the dates for all impacted worlds."

The silence broke with alarm and shouts.

"Master of Fourth Strand needs immediate attention of the higher strands along with science and medical strands equal in stature," the calm voice cut through, making silence fall again.

"Master of Science Fourth Strand listening," preceded a moment before, "Master of Medical Fourth Strand listening."

Ziz-ka's mandibles moved to a more respectful position as the next voices spoke, "The Web, all sectors listening."

He noted Agata hunched once the Web identified themselves. He made a reminder to speak with her later, hopefully when she recovered.

Bron tapped a bottle, which made Agata drink.

"Information shared," the master of the Fourth Strand spoke, "Military strategists agree with assessment of pattern of the worlds. Note the extended pattern applied from last battle with Zinxirs."

The additional pulsing worlds near the cluster they had wasn't a surprise, however two other clusters appeared in different sections of Aqu-jio controlled space.

Agata whispered in horror, "Are samples available?"

"Sciences is assessing based on your pattern, Chief of Medical Staff Agata," the Master of Science Fourth Strand replied.

Lorth's voice made all those around the table turn, "May I sit next to my partner?"

Ziz-ka moved sideways, "Of course, Chief of Medical Staff Lorth."

Lorth set down a box before Agata, "When you are ready, here are some nutrient rich packs."

Agata mutely nodded.

Lorth switched over so his voice was set for Aqu-jio translation only, "If this session takes more than four hours, I will insist on Agata being allowed to take her sleep break. She's skipped many of them pursuing this pattern."

"Why does she need nutrient rich packs?" The Master of Medical Fourth Strand inquired with concern.

"A male human encroached on her person, resulting in the first human hiss," Lorth settled next to Agata, "This is after she missed six meals, and three sleep periods while working with the lab techs on sample matching. I'll speak with the human Lieutenant Commander as to the correct procedure to calm human females in the future."

The other Aqu-jio didn't show a reaction to the statement, but again Ziz-ka and Lorth were the two closest males to Agata.

"Noted," the Master of the Medical Fourth Strand then spoke to Agata, "Is there additional information we need to know on your approach, Chief of Medical Staff Agata?"

She hesitated, then inhaled before saying, "The reason I started looking at these patterns was because I hoped to create a cure from those samples that matched at or near one percent with the zombie plague. Even if it wasn't perfect, it may end the plague."

The Master of the Fourth Strand hummed, "We will work with Science strands on identifying the pieces and cure segments. Your web caught this where ours didn't, but now it is found, we all will get it solved. Your communication strand has our direct lines added."

Ziz-ka spoke, "We have the portions for science and medical divided up, however, our military is bound in the web due to the containment. They cannot take action against the Zinxirs until the plague is addressed fully."

"The Web concurs. Our ships cannot bring this plague outside our containment. It is very contagious and we may risk species outside our view. What options are available for the military strand?"

They discussed, tearing down those plans which violated the containment protocols.

In a silence between plans, Agata stated, "Why can't you use the pico bots to put clean versions of the military members on ships that haven't come into contact with the plague?"

Ziz-ka turned to her, noting her meal boxes laid empty, "What do you mean?"

Lorth picked up the intent, "You mean utilize the remote connected pico bots medicals use to examine individuals in isolated places, yes?"

"I heard from Daniel, who's helping the Vish-Tarin, his modified pico bot body is as functional as the medical ones without the down side of matching pain should it take damage. He's lost six bodies so far without repercussions to his mental nor physical states," Agata looked around, "You can staff your empty ships using the containers of pico bots that is required under the medical statutes to be on board every vessel."

Ziz-ka picked up the plan and enhanced it, "We can add any number of pico bot containers to the ships using the automated ship builders."

The Master of Fourth Science Strand illuminated a problem, "The relays for such control are not designed for multiple individuals using the system over great distance. We'll need to add hundreds if not thousands to each ship. It will limit space for supplies."

Lorth countered, "Pico bots from the medical containers are energized through electrical currents in the containers and their surroundings. We wouldn't need to send in food and liquids. That could free up space and weight for the relays."

"As much as I despise the idea I'm about to put forward, we can also remove the food care-takers' supplies and the pods for growing food. Based on our calculations, we'd have enough weight returned to cover the addition of the relays and pico bot containers without significant lost to the ships," Master of Fourth Science Strand replied.

"The time to make those modifications on our stored ships is weeks at the minimum," Ziz-ka pointed out, drawing on his vast experience, "The Zinxirs won't wait long to take advantage."

"The Web, sector eighteen, the data so far is enough to open an investigation, but not enough to warrant death. We don't know how these...biological weapons were deployed, much less when. Zinxirs are practical creatures. The zombie plague's known spread and speed would be costly to them. They may not be the source of it."

Ziz-ka tapped his legs in irritation.

"A created biological weapon could be created to not infect it creators, or be time-delayed so they could get clear," Agata muttered, "A game from the Second Dark Age required a plague to stay hidden so it could infect everyone, then turn lethal to beat being cured by alerted authorities."

Lorth chittered in concern, "My partner needs to take her rest."

Bron countered, "She may be onto the key."

"Explain?" The Web, sector eighteen demanded.

She typed quickly, then nodded, "Here are the species who visited all identified worlds in the five years previous to their destruction, or travelled near it," the lists were massive as they appeared, "When I apply a search for commonalities, notice the shifts in color."

Ziz-ka swore, as the lists showed multiple yellowed items for partial matches across all the worlds, yet only one green full match. Every list had the same name: Zinxir.

"According to this, some of these weapons could have been deployed up to two years previous to the first sign," Bron turned to Agata, "How would you do it, Agata?"

Agata stared at the lists, her lips pursing, before obvious conflict tore across her face.

"I'm biased, ethically," she choked on the next words, "I was nearly killed by a Zinxir. I..."

Bron gripped her hand, spoke calmly, "Leave the ethics and what happened to you aside for a moment. How would you accomplish this?"

Ziz-ka knew Bron would be promoted soon. She showed the signs of needing the next level of challenges. Her ease with working with a distraught medical and the higher ranks proved she needed promotion before she grew bored.

A part of him would mourn the breaking of their partnership, but then he'd get a new partner. Continuing the cycle for others who would be his partner one day.

Agata blew out a breath, looked at the lists, "Capsules that dissolve over time. Earth used such for medications for at least fifty years before pico bots replaced them."

"No one would trust a Zinxir's capsule. Most would assume poison or some other vile death."

Agata shook her head, "Depending on the material used, they could be placed so water running over it would wear the coating away.

They could have been crushed, like underfoot. During the Second Dark Age, old style land mines were modified to release poisonous gas when someone stepped on them with just the right pressure to breach their containers. Silent, odorless, and tasteless agents of mortality. They still are pulling...they were pulling leftover mines when the zombies outbreak started."

Bron growled, "The old regime of my homeland used that to kill marching protestors. It sparked backlash once the devices were uncovered."

Ziz-ka felt the weariness from Agata as strongly as the rage from Bron.

He startled at Captain Garcia's frigid determination, "They could have left a satellite behind to crash to the surface. If the weapon was sequestered inside sufficient shielding, it would survive the landing and be released. My great-great-grandfather developed such weapons during the Second Dark Age. He committed countless war crimes with that and others like it."

"If these were truly crafted weapons, why did it escape our protocols?" The Master of the Science Strand muttered, "If we had a hint of it being unnatural, it would have been flagged."

Agata growled, making Ziz-ka tense, "That I can answer: You looked at the species records to see if the biological vector was recorded. It's why you all ignored my insistence zombies didn't really exist. You all said 'look at your zombie movies. Obviously you've had such zombie plagues before.' What if that is part of their disguise?"

Lorth's mandibles rubbed, "I do see process notes on at least twenty worlds we researched local medical records. All found a match with the weapon used."

Bron stood, her voice sharpening, "The shared information strands. Did those have such records available for review?"

"Historical and medical shared strands have those same records I reviewed," Lorth confirmed, "What does this mean?"

"Zombie movies and records were the first items added to the shared strands from Earth. A prankster thought uploading supernatural items first would make Earth seem like a horrid place to visit. Those strands are available to everyone, including the Zinxirs, right?" Bron acted like the prankster should have gotten more punishment than what they got.

Ziz-ka laughed, "They found what they wanted but didn't check the truth of it."

Agata grumbled, "Considering there were only four races you have listed as prone to exaggeration, lies and falsehoods, they would have assumed it was truth."

"Science Strand confirms shared strands were accessed by known associates of the Zinxirs. No direct accesses by them."

"The Web, sector eighteen, withdraws objection. I am convinced we have enough information to warrant war and death."

"Which brings us back to retrofitting the fleets in storage will take weeks, even if we alert our impacted allies for help."

Garcia countered, "You can build new fleets in a couple of days. I visited one of your build platforms. You just print the ships out on a super-efficient assembly line. Reconfigure them for new designs and you'll have those ships ready when we are."

Everyone stared at him, then each other.

"The design will need more electrical outputs to keep the pics bots charged, but we could begin construction soon. Once the simulations have checked integrity, we'll be ready for mass production," The Master of the Science Strand commented, "Fleet will be completed in approximately one week."

"We'll begin training for all military members to use the relays. Programmers have been requisitioned. We target one week for deploy of fleet as well," the master of the Fourth Strand stated.

"The Web will append highest priority to all orders related to this."

Agata muttered, "Parasites."

Lorth's leg gently touched her back, "You need rest. You've missed too many."

She looked up at him, her eyes blinking just like Bron's when she had to sleep, words slurring, "Zinxirs would profit from para...parasitical species and abandoned worlds," she rattled off a number of names Ziz-ka recognized but didn't understand why she mentioned them, "Black market or something like it, maybe, cost effective for live humans."

Lorth froze, "How many of those devastated worlds did the Zinxirs claim after? Were any humans taken off their worlds via Zinxir ships prior to the outbreak?"

"You think they are profiting off those species that use others as incubators?" The master of the Science Strand asked for clarification, "Most of those species would use the human waste systems or the female sexual organs. Some could work in conjunction at the same time if this is truth."

"Add that to the worlds they could claim and mine, there's the profit they would desire," the Web, sector eighteen gave a low rumble of displeasure, "We are more than covered for action."

"Agata, you need to rest now. You're stumbling over your words."

Bron stood, "I'll take her back to her quarters. If an escort can be made, it would alleviate concerns of our residents."

Ziz-ka reached out to the security detail outside, confirmed they would help, "They stand ready now. Corridors are cleared."

After they left, Ziz-ka turned back to the communication array, "What would you like for the station to do in the meantime?"

"High Guard of the Web," a new voice broke in, "I recommend a dis-information campaign. We have to assume there is at least one spy who reports to the Zinxirs. They used it during the last war and I doubt they would abandon such tactics when their worth kept them from losing until we...lied to the majority."

Ziz-ka hated the truth in such strategies, "What would you recommend to the information we share?"

"A possible cure has been discovered. All strands are working to disperse the cure via newly built drone ships to prevent further contagion. It won't work on some allies since we will be using their scientists and medicals to craft the real cure. They may see the pattern since we must share the algorithm used to craft our cure. Many of them lost trading partners, loyal allies, and resource sharing agreements due to these biological weapons. The sooner we get them into our web, the better we can entangle our prey with our combined might."

They thought on that for a while, then the Web stated, "Proceed with the mis-information campaign. Fill the shared strands with them and ensure the allies of the Zinxir access them. We'll be prepared for the questions from our allies who either realize the pattern in the cure, or in the dis-information we will lay out as bait. Proceed with all safety. Once the Zinxirs realize we have found their plot, they will be more vicious than at the end of the last war with them. We will eliminate them entirely this time so they never tear our webs again."

Ziz-ka chirred, "This time, they'll think they are killing us, but they'll be killing pico bots instead. I look forward to when they realize we've taken no casualties in the upcoming battles."

Lorth gravely corrected, "If we look at this war they've waged over the centuries, we've suffered more causalities than they ever will."

With that morbid reminder, they broke to start their campaign to turn the war around.

Chapter 29
Spies and Factories

He stared at the feeds from the six automated factories he'd breached.

New ships were being built at top speed.

It had started with one two days ago, then tests.

He recognized the standard space faring exams the Aqu-jio did to ensure they not only survived what ever journey they needed to take, but they would carry even the most fragile cargo and passengers to their destinations without issue.

Except there was something wrong with these ships.

He couldn't place the exact issue since the assembly ran far too quickly for him to review it easily.

To have six factories at various points in the territory the Aqu-jio spanned all working on the same ships meant a massive movement.

Checking the shared feeds, smirking at the strands where all species lambasted the vile humans for bringing the plague into the universe, he scanned for new information.

Chills ran down his chitin, creeping under his plates.

"Cure found, ships preparing for dispersement."

Clacking in irritation, he knew his cut of the bounties from the Zinxirs was in danger.

Checking the counts of the humans, he eased back.

The percentage of offspring carriers was well below the level the Zinxirs wanted. Including ten new deaths he hadn't seen before. Natural deaths from old age.

Arrogant and stupid fleshy humans didn't deserve even one carrier to live, but having so few would have to do.

Assured the humans would die out, he reviewed the cure information being shared.

All the normal science and medical groups signed off on the information. He could see the activity passing through the strands the Aqu-jio used for high-level communications. He dared not try to listen in as that would alert them to his presence.

Drone ships to disperse the cure.

It meant once they confirmed the plague was eradicated, the remaining humans would attempt to reclaim their worlds.

Only they didn't have enough remaining population to keep it for long.

He opened his secure line to his Zinxir contact.

Rox appeared, "You have something worth my time?"

"The Aqu-jio are deploying a cure using drone ships. All the factories are running at full capacity. Consistent activity with when they helped the Vish-Tarin with their mold reactions fifty-seven years ago."

"Hmph. Within the lower boundaries of the timelines we predicted. I hoped they would take longer," the cold eyes narrowed, muzzle wrinkling, "How soon could they deploy the cure?"

"The pico bot vats are being loaded as soon as they are made. If they are going for a whole web deployment, three to four weeks, at least based on the current factories. If they add the non-Aqu-jio factories working on the same designs, two weeks to three before they deploy."

"Anything else?"

"Ten human carriers died since of old age. The species only lasts a century and half before dying, even with pico bots," he clacked with derision.

"Can you add a tracking beacon to the ships?"

He scuttled sideways then back, "Need appropriate motivation."

Rox tapped something off screen.

His accounts registered a massive influx of solid bubbles. The conversion systems worked well.

"I'll send the transmission lines," he disconnected before Rox could.

It would irritate the Zinxir, but if he didn't do it, Rox would take that as permission to hunt him.

They only respected strength and bravado.

He settled to use all his legs to code beacons and add them to the drones during assembly.

Carefully burrowing into the deepest codes, he thought no one would notice his changes.

His arrogance would be the first mistake in the coming war.

Chapter 30

Flight

Daniel leapt over the out cropping, having memorized the path for another sixteen kilometers.

On his back, Sylosh gave commentary for the new section they would try.

Excited he could be outside, even if by remote, he dodged the fierce flora vines that tried to lash out at him, but missed.

He wasn't losing this body to it again, if he could help it.

Though if he did, the latest change to the pico bots to morph from a remote body to remote science drones that monitored the creatures it was absorbed into would prove valuable.

He ducked under an over hang, crawled though a tunnel to the other side.

Here is where the known became unknown.

Carefully, he moved left this time, not right.

To the right was a stationary, multi-armed creature that looked like a spiky starfish.

Left was the new path.

Climbing the path, Daniel smirked at the view to the right.

A deathly drop into a canyon straight down, but out in the distance was a strange mound, rising from the canyon center all the way up to the steep side. Narrow bridges stretched over to edges of the canyon walls, looking rather like they were built than formed.

"Can we get closer to that mound? I want to taste it."

Daniel smirked, "You do know doing so destroyed the sixth set of bodies when you tried to eat the vines, right?"

The whole reason the Vish-Tarin couldn't explore the world came from their absorption properties.

They covered interesting materials and compounds to ingest them, then move on. Only this world turned out to be so tasty, they barely left the area around their base.

Being human, his body didn't automatically absorb where his skin touched other items. He could travel for hours without slowing to munch on whatever caught his eye, unlike his partner. His partner wanted to stop every few feet to snack and taste.

"I want to taste it," Slyosh patted his shoulder, "Maybe worth it like all others, once we figure out how to bypass defenses."

Daniel moved upward, getting closer to the bridge.

He paused before it, kneeling.

Picking up a rock, he tossed it to land in the center.

Then he gaped as the whole bridge snapped on it like a Venus fly trap.

It rippled a moment, then it opened back up.

The rock was gone.

"Still want to taste that?" He asked with amusement.

"Maybe later," Slyosh creeped higher on Daniels nape and shoulders, "The mound is the center of this mass. Look, it draws its food to the underside then pulls or pushes it towards the mound."

Watching the pulling and wriggling underside, he blew out a breath.

"Can we not have this eat us?" He asked, then turned as a shadow passed overhead.

Something dug into his shoulder, making him yelp in surprise.

Then they were airborne.

The flying creature looked like a kite with trailing tendrils like octopus arms. An arm gripped his back, the suckers digging in.

"Tasty," Slyosh rushed up the creature's legs, his color flashing into the deep green his kind did when attacking.

Daniel gripped the arm, worried he was about to be dropped.

A shriek filled the air, echoing off the canyon walls.

He held on as the arm tried to toss him, shaking as the creature twisted, barrel-rolling in an attempt to shake Slyosh.

Then it shuddered, leveled out.

"My mass now," Slyosh's body expanded, creeping over the creature, "Like structure. I'll mimic on next outing."

Daniel made a huge sigh, "We are going into the mound?"

"Yes. Coming up on break, anyway. Good way to end session," the creature dove down at the mound.

Daniel shook his head as they arrowed towards an opening in the side of the mound, "I rather not mass with something like this."

"Next time we mass with something you want to," Slyosh's colors reflected amusement.

Daniel laughed as their bodies slipped through the opening, then they hit something.

They tumbled, the world twirling as Daniel was knocked free.

Then his body was crushed, jerking him back to his quarters.

Shaking his head, he reached up to the apparatus supporting his body like his favorite game system, he disconnected.

Stretching, he walked out of the room the Vish-Tarin, Aqu-jio and six other species designed for him.

It worked better than the one he used on Earth.

Slyosh attached himself to the ceiling outside the quarantine wall.

Daniel didn't mind he was still in isolation. He didn't feel it when he could run and leap outside.

"Slyosh, I really would like to keep a body intact for more than a session. It would be more scientifically beneficial."

"Mass on base happy!" Slyosh cheered without shame, "Sharing of tastes welcomed. We have way to travel faster."

Daniel leaned on the wall, "I think you just like eating too much."

"Not possible to eat too much. This world not enough."

Chuckling, Daniel asked, "So what is my meal today that you all will be enjoying as well?"

"Beef burritos with green chili according to the schedule. Your mother recommended the seasonings."

"Which means spicy hot. You sure you want to try it?" Daniel asked.

"Some of mass loved heat, others not much. Very divided. We will try it."

"Have the oil ready," he had to bite back his amusement his mother's cure for 'Oh god, it's burning my tongue' was so popular with the Vish-Tarin.

"We have vats prepared. Enjoy. We come back after you sleep."

Daniel bade his partner farewell, then walked over to his dining area.

A sealed container sat ready for him.

Cracking the seal, he inhaled.

Then sighed in happiness.

He loved his mom's recipes, missing them as much as their chat sessions.

The first bite made him grin foolishly.

Pulling up the news for his weekly review, he scanned for any cool science articles.

"Cure found, drones being prepared to deal with zombie plague."

He choked, cleared his throat.

A cure?

He read the article and the linked ones.

The Aqu-jio finally identified the plague and developed a cure which worked in both a laboratory setting and a trial run with real subjects. They would have drones deliver the cure to all impacted worlds.

Then he grinned foolishly at the names credited with the discovery.

His mom's name atop the list.

"Keep being amazing, mom," he bowed his head, giving thanks for her efforts, "You will be our savior."

Then he paused.

He checked the numbers of the remaining humans.

Felt his stomach drop.

There was no way traditional human reproduction would bring them back from extinction.

He wasn't great at the medical side, not like his mom, but he dove into the strands for reproductive options.

Slowly, his stomach returned to its normal position.

Hope lived.

Knowing his mom, she'd make sure all those options would be made available to the remaining humans, including access to the vast genetic warehouse the Aqu-jio kept on Aqu-jio Four. Millions of human genetic samples waited to be used.

"Thank you Aqu-jio for being great and collaborative allies," he whispered, then he switched over to the gaming strands, enjoying his meal.

He lost himself in discussions on human gameplay and archetypes.

Chapter 31

Bastion Down

Charles McDonnell sipped his tea, the expensive hand-tended, hand-picked blend savory for its deep richness.

Rowan gave a report on the latest failure to cure the plague.

Fortunately, the zombies above ground looked to be dying out, more and more bodies simply falling and not getting back up.

He had to admire the Zinxirs for their ability to wage espionage on a species level. Collapse the species behind the business, you could then dominate the business without rivals.

A neat solution to a problem his family had diligently worked to master on their worlds.

Once they rose from the rotting corpses of the powerless, he'd employ it against his rivals, adjusted for a uniquely human style.

Rowan coughed, "What?"

Charles looked up to see Rowan's hand covered in blood.

Rowan's eyes rose to his, blood filled just as crimson spilled from his ears.

He collapsed.

Charles stood, backed away, thinking Rowan had infected himself.

Then he coughed.

Blood splattered down his front.

He hit a button, demanded, "Medical to my office."

Only for silence to answer him.

"Security, locate medicals and bring to my office."

Nothing.

Then the door to his office slid open.

Two beautiful women, one with glowing green eyes, the other electric blue, entered without permission.

"I didn't call for you."

"No one will answer your commands ever again," electric blue sneered.

Green eyes smirked silently.

He jolted as Rowan's body began seizing, blood soaking his clothes and the carpet with his jerky movements.

"You thought yourself a king," Blue eyes purred, the sinister tone taking up all the space in the room.

Green eyes moved so she could look down on Rowan, in view of the man if he could see.

He'd seen recordings of his meetings where he cut down competitors or disloyal employees enough to recognize the expressions on the women. Like sharks going in for the killing bite.

Except he was the seal instead of another shark.

"What did you do?" He demanded, spitting out blood.

Blue eyes' vicious smile made him shake inside, "Ancient kings knew to have a taste tester. But even then, they couldn't prevent all poisons."

Green eyes chuckled, "You forgot to secure the pest control. Especially with all it's warnings. The would-be king dies."

"We are the last of humanity. You are killing our species," he tried to reason with them as he stumbled back against display shelves.

"If our species," blue eyes spat icily, "is going to have such a king as you to lead it after all you've done, we deserve to die."

Green eyes kicked Rowan over, death claiming the scientist while they talked, "Humanity was killed by you when you trusted the Zinxirs. Every normal person knows they can't be trusted. But you did. You let our species down with your greed."

His hands settled on one of his most prized possessions, handed down since his great-grandfather's time: a semi-automatic gun.

Blue eyes held up a magazine, "We ensured you won't be using that."

Green eyes held up a single bullet, "Including the one in the chamber."

He coughed, blinking back the red tinge creeping on his vision, "You would have been queens."

"No. Your wife wouldn't have allowed that. Didn't you know she killed the two women you'd been using. She found out they were pregnant. She was too jealous to let their babies come to term," Blue eyes chuckled mirthlessly, "Good thing I had my tubes tied with an off the books doctor. You never did check my body over, only my medical records."

Green eyes snorted as she moved around Rowan's body, "I wish I thought of that. Unfortunately, this baby isn't going to be born."

"The law," he started angrily at her implication.

"The law doesn't matter anymore," Green eyes smirked, "You killed all the cops who'd arrest us."

Blue eyes added, "You destroyed the prosecutors that would bring the case to the court."

"You annihilated the judges who'd rule on the case and render judgement," Green eyes patted her stomach, "If you hadn't, maybe this child would be born. But you set us on this path."

He stumbled, his legs shaking as cold sweat trickled down his neck.

"You took away our humanity with your cruelty," Green eyes knelt out of range.

The next instant his knees hit the carpet, jolting pain through him.

Blue eyes sat cross-legged, "So we took all of your sick sycophants out, poisoning slowly over time, measured so when one dropped, the rest would follow shortly."

"Leaving you last of your company. Once you're dead," Green eyes displayed the bullet, "We get the easy way out."

He sputtered, spraying blood, "I own you."

Blue eyes pulled out some papers, showed him the mark.

"Your legal advisor tried to bribe us out of killing him. All legal," she extended the word with shit-eating grin, "claims to us ended four hours ago. All debtors you took for your trophies are free."

Green eyes laughed when he fell to his side, gasping, "They all died in their sleep, mercifully. Your minions died awake, except two who were further along than we wanted. Your empire falls with you penniless."

He shivered, his body convulsing.

"You die a fake king. We die as real women."

He gripped the carpet, tried to crawl to them.

Only for his grip to lock on the carpet.

Wheezing, the last thing he saw was the women coldly waiting for him to expire.

Chapter 32

New Routines

Agata had been placed on medical leave for four days, her meals delivered like clockwork so she ate three meals each day.

Captain Garcia gave her an ultimatum: follow the regimented schedule the female Aqu-jio did when they hissed, or be relieved of duty.

She hadn't the heart to tell him the threat was unnecessary. She regretted hissing at Gregory as soon as she gotten to the archive.

On the flip side, she was getting a close up and personal view of how the Aqu-jio handled volatile females.

Agata used station water provided through her sink to keep her hydration at appropriate levels between meals.

A caretaking Aqu-jio would deliver her meal, then wait until she finished it in her quarters. Then they'd record it for the station records before taking the empty container away.

Then shortly before her rest period should start, they'd come back to herd her to bed, staying until she fell asleep.

In the morning, a message would alert her Captain Garcia signed off on the previous day, acknowledging she'd completed her meals and sleep period as ordered.

As much as she could feel ashamed at the treatment, she knew if no one watched her, she'd obsess over the cure, going right back to missing meals and sleep.

Once upon a time, her son helped keep her grounded. She would stop to take care of him, even when her work demanded more of her than there were hours in a day.

With humanity on the brink of extinction, she and other women would be pressured into giving birth at every opportunity.

Except the traditional methods would doom her race within two centuries, if not sooner.

Lack of diversity with the remaining humans would consign them to history, unless they used alternative methods.

Even if she wasn't allowed to help the lab techs or Lorth, she could help.

Pulling up the medical articles on available reproduction, she jolted at the video message taking over her screen, hiding the articles.

"Mom, don't worry about this," Daniel's smiling face filled her screen, "I already put in the request for available solutions so you don't have to, at least on this topic. Lorth told me about your leave, so seriously, take a break. I don't want to hear about you regressing on your recovery."

Rubbing her neck, flinching at the raised scars, she sank into her chair.

She switched over to a new book Lorth recommended for her, but with the plague, she'd been distracted.

Trying to make sense of the Aqu-jio mystery novel, she yelped when her door signaled for entry.

Glancing at the clock, she slumped, "Come on in."

Looking over, she smiled at the caretaker Aqu-jio skittering in.

"Your meal from the social hexagon," it gracefully slid a box from the carrier under its body, setting it on her table, then added a bottle, "Lieutenant Commander requested this addition, with Lorth's approval."

Curious, Agata cracked the bottle.

Green tea and chocolate shake.

She paused, flinched at remembering the poison Gregory attempted to slip her in her drinks. She'd been drinking from her sink since he started it, "Lorth checked this?"

"Why do you ask?"

Pinching the bridge of her nose, debating on if she should follow the rules that said certain substances shouldn't be reported to law enforcement, or not.

"We have another law issue from Human Prime," she gritted out.

"Is that why you insisted on using station water?"

Nodding, she added, "This law applies to both genders equally, but it's vile for being a law."

The care-taker tapped the station communication strand, "Request law review."

Sitting forward, Agata prepared for a difficult situation.

Captain Stefan Garcia, Doctor Karmal Landris and Bron appeared, along with Lorth and Ziz-ka.

Ziz-ka chortled, "Why are there so many laws that foolishly punish your race?"

Wincing, Agata simply stated, "Second Dark Age."

"I second that assessment," Stefan rolled his eyes, "Our ancestors were very, very barbaric."

"What is of concern?" Bron asked calmly.

Agata rattled off the exact law, "I was under the influence of a drug with the street name Whorish Date while married to my ex-husband. When I entered rehab, I was told detox and withdrawal would be difficult. Unfortunately, I'm one of those who has an adverse reaction in the addiction category. If I take another dose, it could retrigger my dependency or worse. As in fatal."

Bron looked to the side, pursed her lips, "The law also lists you cannot report whoever may be using these drugs."

"Jail time of no less than six months if I report the drug being used against myself or another person."

"I recognize these symptoms," Lorth's mandibles flared, "I've had to treat several women and two men on station for this. The lab couldn't confirm the source of the symptoms."

"Whorish Date is designed to leave no traces after ingestion."

"How did you know someone was using it against you?"

Agata pulled out the case with the last test strip, "I purchased a kit for testing the presence of it in a drink before posting here. I got in the habit of testing drinks once I was back to my quarters. In the last three months, all my drinks have tested positive. It's why I switched to station water. The station's filtration systems would prevent it from reaching me, even if someone was stupid enough to poison us all."

"I vote to have this law stripped from the books," Bron stated cooly.

Doctor Landris rubbed her face, "I'm of the mind to strip out all laws and implement the Aqu-jio ones. I do not have the inclination nor temperament to go one by one through them."

Garcia looked pained, "I have to abstain from this vote."

Agata hung her head, knowing why he said so instantly, "Same for me."

"Do we really need a third vote?" Ziz-ka asked.

Lorth interrupted, "I interject that as the Aqu-jio Chief of Medical Staff, I can override any law should it prevent me from treating or saving any life on board, even to permanently strike it down. The implications of this for those who have vulnerable systems to it side-effects, leads me to vote for full removal, as detailed under our treaties."

"I do believe we have our decision. Agata, with the removal of this law, can you detail who is doing this?"

Agata let her shoulders relax, "I know of one, but there could be more. Gregory."

Stefan growled, "That is why you hissed at him, isn't it?"

"Partly. He's been pestering me for sex for some time. I think this drug was an attempt to push pass my resistances," It felt good to have it in the open.

"Would you test your drink please?" Bron added a mini video, "He was there when the bartender prepared her shake."

Selecting the tweezers from the case, she gripped the test strip then dipped it fully into the shake.

When she pulled it free, the strip had changed from white to red.

"Positive," Agata capped the shake, handed it over to the caretaker, "I can't have this."

The caretaker rumbled dangerously as it packed the bottle away, "No one interferes in my duties."

Lorth blew out a breath, "And mine. I request Gregory is arrested and placed in the brig. I'll pull the other victims and see if we have other perpetrators who need to be taken in for disturbing the operation of our station."

"Pass them along to me," Ziz-ka rubbed his mandibles in glee, "I think security needs more practice in capturing humans and transporting them."

"Just don't harm them so much I have to treat them," Lorth commented dryly, "I have enough to do without adding dubious burdens to it."

"Could he have gotten this drug into the food?" Stefan asked.

Agata looked at the strip, then the container, "It's usually a drink."

The caretaker took the container, then collected the used strip, "I'll have the bartender prepare a fresh version."

"Thank you," Agata hung her head.

A leg touched her shoulder, making her look up at the caretaker.

"Your hissing was valid. He deserved to be eaten."

Then the caretaker scurried out.

Agata gave a soft chuckle at the support.

"Any other laws lurking out there we need to address now?" Stefan asked.

Emboldened, Agata raised her head, "Reproduction when an individual is not infertile being limited to traditional methods."

Lorth waved a leg, "Remove. Your species will die out with such a law allowed to stand."

Ziz-ka asked, "Why was this law allowed?"

Agata joined Stefan, Docter Landris, and Bron in saying, "Second Dark Ages."

"I withdraw my question. Is it better to assume that era is the source of so much pain?"

Bron folded her arms across her chest, "I know where the laws come from. As part of the command sector, I have to know the laws, no matter how much I hate them. You need to take the time to review them, just like I did for yours."

Ziz-ka's mandibles moved for a long moment, before stating, "Are you saying I need to be promoted again since I have more learning to do?"

Bron huffed, "I am not letting you get out of our partnership so easily. I know you put in a recommendation for my transfer to a station closer to Aqu-jio Prime once humans can move freely."

Ziz-ka laughed, "Alright, I will consider your words. Though it may startle a few to have me suddenly promoted after I was demoted."

"Don't use that word!" Bron barred her teeth, "I will stuff your mouth full of peanut butter if you use it again."

"What is peanut butter?" Ziz-ka asked, obviously confused.

Agata swallowed her snicker, "A food paste from Earth known for its ability to glue mouths shut."

"Hmm, I think I have other duties calling," Ziz-ka's screen vanished.

Lorth cautioned, "I've had to release three Aqu-jio from that substance. I beg you to reconsider your punishment, Lieutenant Commander. At least until Agata is back on duty with me."

"Depends on him. Are we all in agreement the reproduction law for traditional is stricken from the law books?"

At the unanimous agreement, Agata breathed a sigh of relief.

"I look forward to working with you on reproduction solutions," Doctor Landris grinned, "I kinda want to try two of them myself."

"Later," Agata leaned back at Lorth's irritated chirr.

They closed the channel to her relief.

When the caretaker returned with her meal, she happily devoured it.

Chapter 33

Shipping Out

The ships the Aqu-jio built began to move out, far sooner than the communication strands stated they should have.

He clacked nervously as the beacons registered their paths, all moving in the same direction.

Programing an algorithm for where they could be going, factoring in margin of error bands the further from their current locations, he waited for his computers to provide their analysis.

Something was wrong.

He checked the strands, confirmed they still listed the cure wasn't deploying yet.

What were the Aqu-jio up to?

His computer clicked its completion of the task.

Bringing up the results to his main display, he froze.

No.

No, no, no.

He tapped the communication strand to Rox.

Only nothing happened.

Desperately, he tried it again. Then again with a frustrated slam.

Why couldn't he reach out to Rox?

His screens went dark, making him scuttle backwards nervously.

"So you were spying for the Zinxirs."

He whirled, raising his claws into fighting position.

Three of his kind and an Aqu-jio entered his home, weapons at full power.

Hissing at them, he replied, "I am no spy."

"Our laws explicitly state working with the Zinxirs to harm us or others means you are a spy. The Aqu-jio shared the strands you tied into their factories to monitor their ship builds and the changes you introduced to track those ships. We traced them back to your computer. Admit your guilt with honor."

He stiffened, "You allowed the humans to claim the world my ancestors visited. You let them despoil the location of their remains."

"What are you speaking about?" The smallest of his kind questioned.

He snapped, "You let them take Crok-Lir 10238A. That was my family's world. You had no right to hand it over to the humans."

The Aqu-jio cocked her head, "The world with that designation was unclaimed by all members. We explicitly checked with all species, including yours."

"His family has never left Crok-Lir Prime. They've refused to serve in the exploration and military divisions that would allow such a claim," the smallest shook his chitin sadly, "Medicals to come forward."

Clacking his claws in anger, he charged them.

They dishonored his ancestors. They lied about the world his ancestors landed on, died on. They would die for the insult.

Shocks froze his limbs, making him tumble helplessly.

He raged as four medicals circled him.

"Mind rot," one stated to the four waiting guards, "Its reached first stage and would make him susceptible to manipulation and override his true memories."

They caged him, then hauled him before he could begin to twitch his limbs.

Staring at the ceiling, he wished he could have warned Rox.

The Aqu-jio ships headed for the Zinxir territories. All of them.

Chapter 34

Crewed

It felt equally familiar and strange as Ziz-ka walked down the ship's corridors.

Familiar from centuries of living on such ships, some headed to war, strange in that it wasn't his real body moving.

The halls were crowded on all four surfaces with scurrying Aqu-jio.

He entered the command deck, pausing beside his partner's doppleganger.

Bron looked up from the map, "Vish-Tarin remote piloted warships have joined with ours. They are the last for this section of the Battle Web."

"I didn't think they had many who were ready for remote piloting."

Bron gave the briefest smirk he'd ever seen on a human, "Daniel Morales' scouting program was picked up by all their worlds. They didn't alert us to their new skill set until yesterday."

"How soon until we enter Zinxir space?"

"A few minutes," Bron straightened, "Are you sure you wanted me on board?"

If he was going to be promoted with her, she needed some experience with warships, "Yes. Humans found their biological weapons, humans could spot their treacheries we are not prepared for."

Bron humphed, "Agata should be on board then. She saw it first."

"Captain Garcia and Lorth have not deemed her fit for duty. She's not been made aware we are launching the attack as yet."

"I would like her to be present when we declare the reason for this attack. They should see the woman who brought their plans into the light and foiled them."

Ziz-ka rubbed his mandibles, then activated the private line to the Fourth Strand.

He relayed the request to the Master of the Fourth Strand for review.

"We will have all human leaders present on your ship. Do make sure they last until the battle begins," the Master of the Fourth Strand then added, "Their females are proving as aggressive as ours when insulted."

"There is a benefit to human females."

"Ohh?"

Ziz-ka chuckled, "Even at their sleepiest and hungriest, they never eat their kind nor ours."

Laughter filled the strand.

He looked over as the containers next to the door opened and dispensed more remote bodies.

Stefan shivered, "This is distinctly unsettling," he turned to Agata, "You do this often?"

Agata looked less beaten down than when he saw her in the archive, "I've had to do twelve back to back sessions, each on separate worlds. Though that was before the zombie plague started."

Doctor Landris touched her hands, "I think I may have a few dozen uses for bodies like these. I will be contacting you in the near future for tips and tricks, Chief of Medical Staff Morales."

"I would refer you to Daniel Morales who is serving as scout to the Vish-Tarin. He has a lengthy list to share," Agata commented as she followed Stefan to the table displaying the Battle Web.

"I've been meaning to ask you about your son. Does he get his intelligence from you or his father?"

"If his father still lived, he'd say it was him," Agata's bitterness made many of the Aqu-jio ease away from her, "However, he takes more after me. What prompted your inquiry?"

"Let's just say I want to work on a project that would benefit from your input," Landris patted Agata's shoulder, then looked over the map as she changed the subject, "I've never been on a warship before. This is fascinating."

Agata sighed, "This would be my second, though previously it was after a battle."

Ziz-ka blinked as Lorth appeared from a container, walked over to stand next to his partner, "If I ask you to disconnect, please do so."

"I take it my normal caretaker is monitoring me?" She asked with amusement.

All the Aqu-jio relaxed.

"She is. I won't have you missing a meal nor sleep period because of this," Lorth gestured to Stefan, "Medical and Command order."

The dry reply made Ziz-ka muffle a laugh, "I'm sure it's backed by higher ranks."

"Entering Zinxir space," Bron announced, following the protocol of the training program Ziz-ka gave her two days ago.

Ziz-ka watched the ships flying in the territory, noting many were from species the Aqu-jio forbade from interactions with humans.

Very few Zinxir ships, which was very suspicious.

They wouldn't leave their borders unprotected.

What was their plan?

"Transmission being broadcast to all of the Battle Web," Bron relayed, turned to the station commander.

"Transmit to our section of the Battle Web," he ordered, "Ziz-ka, I want you on firing strands. I suspect they are going to start this battle."

Ziz-ka eased over to the station, plugging in his suit's communication strand and confirming his command rank.

"This is the Zinxir Consortium. What is the purpose of the ships approaching?"

Ziz-ka hid his amusement as the Web answered.

"The Web has judged the actions of the Zinxir biological attacks on the following worlds and demand recompense," each sector of the Web listed off a subset of the worlds.

"We are not responsible for attacks on those worlds. Demanding recompense for such is invalid. Leave our territory."

The Web stated as one, voices overlapping in icy rage, "Aqu-jio granted you leniency for many crimes during and after the war between us. You paid us back with treachery and death, shredding our web with your viciousness. We will rectify our misplaced faith in you by doing as those harmed by you demanded over the centuries."

"We accept your declaration of war, food."

Ziz-ka jolted as millions of ships suddenly appeared.

Blasts began firing at their ships, rocking them with each blow.

Bron called, "A fifth of our portion of the Battle Web are disabled, another fifth is damaged with half capability."

Ziz-ka gave orders then asked, "How did we miss the ships?"

"Nothing was on sensors until they appeared. A cloaking device?" The commander asked before their ship jerked sideways.

"Do they have space drives that operate faster than ours?" Landris questioned, then yelped as she lost her footing, stumbling into Agata.

Agata braced them both, "Teleportation or a space gate?"

"There is no technology advancements like those announced," the commander rubbed his mandibles in irritation.

Agata growled, "Just like a Zinxir shouldn't have been able to bypass your security? They must have used a small scale version of this when I was attacked."

"Half of our portion of the Battle Web is disabled, the remaining ones are half capability."

Ziz-ka watched only a few Zinxir ships blow up on the enemy side from their barrages, "We need a solution to do more damage to them."

Bron offered, "Call in all the other species."

"That would violate containment protocol," the commander's shocked response filled Ziz-ka with dread, "The Web wouldn't authorize it."

"The Zinxirs wiped out one hundred and twenty-two species since your last war with their biological weapons," Agata countered, "Those impacts radiated through your entire web of allies and trading partners, straining the strands binding them all into one. If you don't call them up, they will see this attack in progress. They will come since they want their piece of the Zinxirs in retribution. While they are coming in, get all existing ships into motion."

Bron added, "We have over sixteen thousand human ships docked at various human stations you've kept under containment until you had enough engines to move them as one unit to their closest stars. We possess the command passwords to have them take off and set into motion. Without humans on board we can unlock the limiters and have them reach highest speed. If we can add explosives to them via remote drones, they can be used as mobile mines. Three quarters of our portion of the Battle Web are disabled, remaining approaching disable status."

Agata touched the commander's leg mirroring the pleading of a lessor officer to a higher ranked one, drawing Ziz-ka's attention as their gunning stations began to go offline, "The Web needs to make a decision. The Zinxir or the entire web of allies they have fostered since you first took to space."

Ziz-ka concurred, "We need their highest order."

Opening the line the commander stated, "The Web has only two options for their web. Our allies survival against an enemy, or the containment. We need this decision now."

"What do you recommend?" The Web asked as one voice.

"Call all our allies, all ships of remote and direct pilot, all fighters to end this threat forever."

Ziz-ka didn't hear the reply as an explosion destroyed their ship.

He jerked in his support web, cursed.

Bron struggled out of hers, rushed to the station's command table, bringing up the distant battle.

The delay was minutes, but they could see the Battle Web fraying under the continuous attack from the Zinxirs.

Ziz-ka leapt free bringing up the communication strands.

Except he didn't need to.

The Web's combined voice echoed from every screen on the command deck, "The Aqu-jio declare the Zinxir as enemies to ourselves and all species in accordance with our treaties. Web containment for the zombie plague is lifted so the perpetrators of it may find their deeds visited upon them."

Ziz-ka waited with bated breath.

"Vish-Tarin mass joins with Aqu-jio in exterminating the Zinxirs for killing our trade partners and allies."

"Hir-zt Nest will support the assault on the Zinxirs. Glad to hear they forsook their second chance."

Voices, thousands of them called their support, growing into a cacophony.

"Ziz-ka, human ships released from their stations, directing them into Zinxir territory," Bron stated typing as fast as she could as her fingers could bear, Stefan matching her speed from his station, "We need explosives added from the factories along the way."

Ziz-ka typed the order, then stated into the strand, "We need any of those in the shadows to act. They must step silently into this battle."

The code words were for the shadowy edges of the web, those who laid in wait with traps and sneaky attacks. He was one of the privileged few to have led them once upon a time.

He hoped they'd move fast. They needed distractions to split the Zinxir fleets.

Bron cursed, "More Zinxir ships appearing on the border where the Battle Web is being destroyed."

Agata's voice called on the station internal strand, "We need a demoralizer."

"What would demoralize a Zinxir?" Bron demanded, "They are the most vicious bastards in the universe."

"Send me all the supernatural records they accessed from the shared strands."

"How will that help?" Bron sent the files through anyway.

Ziz-ka checked the munitions being loaded to the human ships. Forty percent complete.

"They haven't seen us. It's time to make them scared," Agata purred with such malice, Ziz-ka shuddered.

"How?" Bron snapped angrily.

"Review the file I sent you."

Ziz-ka looked over, blinked at the images displayed.

"It looks like you with a weird robe, a fluffy headpiece and your lower body as some sort of snake?" Ziz-ka commented with confusion.

"Oh," Bron breathed, then gave a little jump, "Oh!"

Stefan swiped the image to the next one, Bron with a strange robe bearing some sort of spear-like weapon in her hands and a three headed Zinxir looking creature at her back.

The next was Stefan with glowing red eyes, incisors long enough to make an Aqu-jio proud and white skin. A black and red cape with a high collar completed the look.

Agata's space cold voice made him tap his legs nervously, "They used our records against us. Time to use ours against them."

"What's the plan? How do we get this out to them?" Stefan demanded.

"How fast is a scout ship carrying a single relay and a container of pico bots? Swift enough to get through their firing lines to the ships? Can the pico bots be configured to absorb their energy from Zinxir ships?"

"Ziz-ka?" Bron asked, looking like she had no clue.

"We can get them to the front lines in an hour, not sure on the pico bots," Ziz-ka tapped his legs, "What are you proposing?"

When he heard the plan, he laughed.

Then he ordered up a single factory to retool for multiple breachers, built for speed only. Without organic life on board, they could move more rapidly.

Chapter 35

Monsters From Earth

The Zinxirs chortled as the Aqu-jio incursion was stopped barely inside their border.

Rox sneered, "Weak fools. We can overcome them now."

A holographic image of the oldster scoffed, "Underestimate the Aqu-jio to your doom. They hid this attack from us. They may have other tricks to release from their webs. New weapons or tactics."

"You lost the battle with yourself and them by cowering," Rox howled his laugh at the tight expression on the oldster's face, "They have nothing new to attack us with."

"Incoming fast moving objects," Rox's second in command warned, "They are moving too fast to hit with our weapons."

"Where are they headed and how many?"

"On trajectories with our front line border ships."

Pulling up the image of the ships, Rox laughed, "These are old style breaching missiles. There's no life on them who could board our ships. No threat. Keep our focus on the Aqu-jio ships. Wipe them out."

"We are registering additional ships inbound. Multiple species are represented."

Rox's maniacal bellow filled the room with his confidence, "We break them, we own them all. With the Aqu-jio shattered these others will be on our dinner plates. Prepare to meet them."

"The breaching missiles have struck their targets. Onboard security checking them over," his second relayed, "Ships on the edges are changing targets to new wave of enemies."

Alarms sounded, making Rox twist to his second.

"Border ships are reporting they've been boarded."

"Show me," Rox snapped his teeth, "They must have some sort of jammer for our scanners."

The first ship made him cock his head.

White mist filled the corridor from the floor to the ceiling.

Weapons fired into the mist as a shape grew darker against the whiter droplets.

"I have come to suck your blood."

Strange flying creatures rushed out of the mist, Zinxir yips of pain filling the communication.

Lavender Zinxir blood sprayed, tinting the mist for a few seconds.

Thuds sounded before the flying creatures swarmed back together.

Then coalesced into a human with a cape, black on the outside, red on the inside.

The human male looked up at the camera, smiled. Fangs long enough to be threatening even when barely uncovered sent a tremor though Rox.

"You took my normal...donors," the human's cultured yet sinister rumble made Rox's fur bristle on his nape, "Pity you didn't pay mind to tales of my court."

Three human women drifted from the mist, their skin as pale as the white dresses they wore, save where Zinxir blood soaked them. Their fangs glistened as they licked them.

"My brides and I will enjoy our meal. Do bring more for us to feast on. We hunger."

"Match that human with the records we have," Rox ordered, scanning the other screens.

A human female appeared, pointing on another ship, "Fetch me the souls of the damned. The river Styx could do with a few hundred of these befouled creatures."

A three headed, four footed Zinxir-like creature bayed, charging a group of Zinxirs, shrugging off the weapon fired at it.

Each head bit into different Zinxir, shaking them as Zinxir did prey.

Another showed a human female with a strange four footed body under her torso charging another security team, yelling, "Chiron, my father, I shall avenge you!"

"Matches found. The first ship is identifying the attackers as Vlad the Impaler with his vampire brides. The second matches only on the three headed beast. Cerebus, the hound of Hades, Guardian of the river Styx in the realm of the dead. The third matches on body type as centaur, the name just spoken as the ally of human hero Hercules. They are all human matches from their records."

"That can't be. There would be signs of them before this," Rox fought the panic down as more screens showed more and more impossible human beings.

On one a Zinxir headed, human bodied male raised a scale, "As commanded by Ra, I judge you as unfit."

A strange mixed animal hissed as it stamped by the being, the reptile head frilled by a furry mane.

"We are getting matches from multiple records. Matches are for human deities, monsters, immortals," his second turned, "Our weapons are ineffective on them."

"How?" Rox stared at the chaos, demanding these be illusions, "Earth has no more humans on it."

"Sir, we unleashed the zombie plague. What if by killing the humans with that weapon, we angered the beings those records warned about. Look!" He pointed to a woman with a feathered head dress, slitted eyes, forked tongue and a snake tail instead of human feet, "This one has destroyed our largest border ship by herself. It's listing her as the Mother of the Feathered Serpent. She's the deity of stars and darkness, mother of the god of wisdom and light, Quetzalcoatl. This is her son," the second brought up a more snake-like human, tearing the interior of ship with claws made of light, his deep hisses reverberating off the corridors.

Believing what he witnessed, Rox snapped, "Find their weaknesses. Alert all the others we have monsters from Earth attacking. Prevent them from boarding our ships."

Chapter 36

Playing Along

Daniel enjoyed the character his mother passed to him to play.

The pico bots were programmed to break down damaged bots making up his body, creating new ones in an ever regenerating cycle. They supplemented it by sucking up pieces he sheared from the corridor with his attacks.

He tore apart the Zinxir who faced him, his claws scorching the wounds closed when he hit.

Hissing at his enemies, he flashed his feathered frill, the iridescent scales drawing their gazes in the wrong direction.

Away from his flying winged serpent pet, who was Slyosh in disguise.

Flicking his tongue, he slithered deeper into the ship, tearing into whatever pleased him.

His mom used to tell him stories of the old gods from before the Second Dark Ages. Stories that survived through oral recitation when the backbone of the world wide communication network collapsed.

He loved the ones featuring the spider prankster, Anansi. It was why he insisted on getting a stuffed spider toy when he was little.

One he kept in a box made from fire-proof material so nothing could destroy it and the connection to his mom.

Then he paused as his mother's voice reached him over the communication strand, "These ships can be finished by our allies. Prepare for your exits."

Stefan gave a soft laugh, "Our next locations are ready?"

"Missiles already in place. We won't have a lot of time before they figure out this is a ruse. Countdowns will sound individually. This should keep them spread out."

Daniel smirked at the enemies cowering behind a makeshift barrier, issuing hissing laughter at them.

Their eyes widened as their ears pinned back with their terror.

Slyosh wrapped around his neck before flaring his wings above Daniel's head like an ancient head dress.

Daniel heard the countdown begin on his end as he straightened, digging his claws into the upper part of the walls so he towered over his enemies.

He inhaled on the count of one, then blew out a breath as the pico bots swarmed forward in a blast of fiery light, dissolving his remote body in the process.

Then he began rising from the container on the new ship, Slyosh biting one of the Zinxirs investigating the missile while entangling two others in his coils, squeezing them to death.

Daniel slithered out, then smirked at the new Zinxirs who rushed around the corner.

Mocking them with more hissing laughter he started slaughtering them.

In his mind he sent a message to his mom, "When this is over, we can make some pretty cool games with these remote bodies."

She sent back, "Create a new business later, deal with these mangy mutts now."

The hatred in those words concerned him, so he replied, "What happened?"

When no reply came quickly, he proceeded with his mission, Slyosh sending him information on new enemies before they rushed them.

All those deaths on the Vish-Tarin Forty-Three really paid off on their coordination. He and his partner moved as if they were two dancers among those with two left feet.

It was so easy to do.

He paused at the message his mother sent.

Then rage burned through him.

They hurt her like that. Made her bear her agony without him to support her in her hour of need.

They would suffer for her pain.

Slyosh sent him a question.

"They nearly killed my mother over a year ago. She suffered alone through a pico bot level surgery," Daniel texted his partner even as he roared his anger, vibrating the hallway.

"Mass with me," Slyosh circled his neck, then he felt the powerful mind of his partner mix with his.

Not just his mind.

All the Vish-Tarin.

Awe filled him as they calmed him, so many memories of lost members to the same species submerging his. His mother was one who survived, when most didn't. Their gratitude she lived soothed him.

"Let us strike together as one," the thoughts dulled his own rage into tranquility, "We bring them down as they did us."

Their arms slammed into the walls, the pico bots consuming the metal like acid ate through it. The mass liked using the appearance of melted metal to hide their actions.

Wings sprouted from their back, the colors flashing with glowing brilliance as more enemies charged them.

A wing beat sent them flying, the air like a cannon against them.

"Son," he paused at a message, "I am getting my vengeance, one Zinxir at a time. We will sit after this and talk, really talk."

"We understand," they replied.

Her reply made a rippled of laughter cross the whole mass, "Preferably without the bigger mass. I don't want my recipes getting out so soon."

Slithering forward, they broke the ship to pieces until the countdown sent them to the next ship.

Chapter 37

Old Dogs, New Tricks

The oldster sat back, observing the chaos at the border.

Rox and Jav's forces weren't holding their ground in the face of the new enemies.

Mythical creatures from the humans walked and scoured the border ships, leaving many crippled from the inside.

Tapping his nose with a claw, he looked deeper at the attack.

If these beings had been on Earth the whole time, they could have stopped the plague by eliminating those infected.

Yet the satellites left to monitor Earth registered no remaining humans, untouched or infected.

His second and third stepped up to him, their grizzled and scarred muzzles grim.

"Thoughts?" The oldster asked.

"Strange they are using the missiles to breach the border ships when they seem to teleport between them. Feels...off," his second wrinkled her muzzle, "like they really aren't gods or monsters."

His third growled unhappily, "I feel like we are watching one of those entertainment shows from Earth, the ones that showed poorly done digital manipulation."

The oldster nodded, "Yes. Except these are better made, more real. Are any of ours breached yet?"

"One will be in a few."

The oldster gestured, "Have them deploy an anti-pico bot field around the breach. Maybe they are using medical remotes."

"With the damage they were taking, the mental fortitude is greater than even the Aqu-jio," his third commented as he issued the order, "They would have curled in on themselves by the second security team."

Turning to his second he asked, "How would you accomplish a victory over them?"

"If pico bots are the base, attack the pain receivers. We could amplify it by briefly upping outputs on the anti-pico bot field to different frequencies."

"Do that instead. I want to see if it makes them halt."

He tapped his fingers on his table as the second wave of alien ships met the border ships, trading fire.

Scowling, he spotted two more waves reaching the outermost satellites.

Then he leaned forward as the full scope of those waves filled the view.

"Every species," he muttered, "All of them are coming."

Looking up he stated to his crew, "The Aqu-jio containment has been lifted, prepare for multitudes of enemies to engage us."

"Should we engage?" His third offered caution, "We could slip away and hide."

The oldster scanned the ids of the massive fleets converging on the border, felt the same certainty that made him surrender so long ago confirm in a different direction, "They are planning on exterminating us to the last. We make our final stand. Bring up our weapons."

"We caught one!" His second smirked, "The feathered female."

The figure twisted back from the shots being fired, the grim expression on its face clear to them as it raised its arms to shield it from the weapon fire.

"Pico bots confirmed. Should I change the field to disperse them?"

The oldster smirked, "Let that one suffer. If possible, lock the swarm in place so they can't disconnect from the remote body."

"Should we share with the others?" His second looked displeased with the idea.

"We still have the exterior, middle and interior fleets. Let's see if having one locked dis-spirits the others."

Then his third inhaled sharply, "What?"

The pico bot swarm they'd captured in the field suddenly changed.

Oldster stared at a ghost.

The human female raised her head, her short statue clear compared to their security members.

His grandson told him he killed the human he'd been sent after.

Yet she stood there.

"A ploy," he snarled, fearing his grandson's adult license would be overturned if this wasn't another fake, "They seek to use ghosts now."

"Hello," the ghost spoke with icy calm, "You probably thought I died."

His muzzle wrinkled as she looked at the security forces as if they couldn't hurt her.

"Lix of Breaker via Zinxir Prime failed to kill me," the certainty in the voice made the security members hesitate as she continued, "You know, you should always make sure your prey is dead. Especially when you are doing your first alien kill."

Her eyes shifted so she seemed to be staring at the oldster, her barred teeth clearly a threat.

"Lix of Breaker via Zinxir Prime, your clan has allowed this shame to spread into your honor," her words cut as surely as claws, "Will you send him out to face his prey, or will you cower in your dens?"

The oldster growled, "Search the human records our allies copied. Confirm Agata Morales lived."

He didn't have to wonder how she knew the words of the Zinxirs. He spent centuries studying all the Aqu-jio weaknesses, listing all their assumptions they could use to hide attacks.

She stood there like she knew the Zinxir's ways of life.

A worthy enemy.

Her meat would be tastier for the killing.

"She's confirmed as living. The listing has Lorth performing a pico bot surgery for her. Her partner must have saved her by converting her into a pico bot swarm," his second looked worried, "If Lix doesn't answer this, all of us will be dishonored."

His claws dug into the table, his rage at his inept grandson filling him.

Someone took the human and made her into a pico bot swarm, probably using the same technology she used to assault them on their ships. An advanced medical technique the Aqu-jio only shared with their closet allies. None of the Zinxir's allies and spies ever got close enough to witness it, much less learn it.

"Open a line to this specter," he ordered.

At the nod from his third he rumbled, "Who are you to imply any Breaker would fail to kill their prey?"

When she countered with the perfect Zinxir response, he resisted wrinkling his muzzle, "I'm Chief of Medical Staff Agata Morales, human, Earth ground. The prey designated from the list. I lived while my predator failed."

"Where will you meet your end?" He challenged.

Her eyes glimmered with equal provocation, "Where will Lix of Breaker via Zinxir Prime meet his?"

Snorting at the incongruity of this prey being certain of facing the one who mauled her and winning amused him.

She had bravado.

Silencing the communication, he stated to his grandson, "You left your prey alive."

Lix snorted as he stepped into view, "It's probably her son."

"No," the oldster corrected, "The Aqu-jio records show her partner put her back together. You need to correct this, now."

Lix asked, "Where?"

"Where do you want to do it?"

"In full view of her son," Lix stated.

"Unless one of these other pico bots is her son, choose..."

Lix smiled, pointed, "Like mother, like son."

The snake man rampaging on his fourteenth border ship bore elements of the female form Agata Morales took.

The oldster turned to the screen, triggering the communication open again, "In front of your child."

He shivered at her purr, "Acceptable."

Chapter 38

Fears Revisited

Agata fought the freak out as her son formed next to her, still in his deity form.

His text to her covered her nerves like a balm, "Your strength is better than theirs combined."

"We will see, my son and his numerous partners," she sent back, adding a little smile to it.

"You raised this mass to stand alone, just as you have. You will overpower the enemy mass."

She never thought the Zinxir would face her as the pico bot swarm. She didn't understand what they were thinking.

Didn't they know her body wasn't really here?

Then she watched her nightmare striding towards her. Taller, leaner than she remembered, with a scar bisecting his nose, yet still clearly him. Lix.

She looked at her son, then looked to the side.

Getting the non-verbal request, he slithered backwards, a smirk on his snake face, eyes locked on the approaching Zinxir.

"You were weak before," Lix commented as he came to stop, "Do you think you can handle me, human?"

A thought crossed her mind, another supernatural creature which haunted humanity's mind since before the First Dark Age. One ideally suited to facing her enemy since it was human only part of the time.

"I'll face you with the form you didn't allow me to take before."

She grew in size to match him, fur sprouting from her skin as her nose and mouth merged into a muzzle, claws extending from her fingers as her muscles thickened.

His expression froze, "You can't be serious."

Letting out the part of her that could lie, and do it well, from its slumber since she divorced her husband, she cocked her head, "You unleashed a zombie plague that put the one which decimated Earth during the First Dark Age to shame. Did you really think zombies were the only creature to cause problems on Earth? Shape-changers are as common as the undead. It enables us to live a little longer through fatal damage since you used nothing I am vulnerable to," she mocked him, "Long enough for a skilled Aqu-jio to restore me to who I am."

"Werewolf, weak predator of Earth," Lix sneered, "So how is it you are forcing this change without a full moon?"

"If I changed at every full moon like my ancestors, the humans would have found me out, discovered my son. That would be weak. Fortunately, our wills are stronger than those before us," Agata sent Daniel a text of what she wanted him to do.

His pico bot swarm changed into his human form, then morphed into a black furred version of herself.

"Lock them into this form," Lix ordered.

Agata felt the field that forced her to feel pain shift like a cold breeze through her being.

She dodged to the side, Lix's swipe slow to her eyes.

Her backhand sent him back two steps.

He laughed, "Weak."

Ducking under his next slash, going to her knees, she dug her claws into his thigh, tore.

He yelped, leapt backwards.

She barred her teeth, lifting up the chunk of meat she held, "Weaker."

He cocked his head, "You don't move like a human."

Tossing the meat to the side, she sneered, "You move as slow as them."

Circling, pacing on all four paws, she watched him.

This time he'd end up on the floor bleeding out, not her.

"You strike my mother to help him," Daniel's growl rumbled past her and her enemy, "I will show you how a wolf pack destroys interlopers."

The voice which asked her where she wanted to face her nightmare snarked, "You and what weak pack?"

Agata chuckled darkly, "Why do you think so many supposed humans survived?"

She sent a text out, taking a chance.

Lix slashed at her.

She lunged under his arms, rose up to snap her teeth on his muzzle, the crunch along with his yowl satisfying.

He twisted, flinging her against the wall.

Pain lashed her, but she'd survived worse. So much worse.

Licking her chops, she snapped her teeth at him, growling darkly.

He looked past her, froze with shock.

Bron's voice rumbled ominously, "One pack."

"Honorable, or meat?" Stefan howled, pitching his voice two octaves down.

The Zinxir behind Lix looked close to panic, save the old one with the most scars.

His eyes switched from one spot to another behind Agata.

"Who is Agata Morales to you?" The old one narrowed his eyes.

Lorth's text crossed her mind, "The human ships are nearing the border. Ziz-ka estimates he packed enough to destroy half the Zinxir fleet. ETA seven minutes to detonation."

Doctor Landris' voice dryly replied, "Alpha, obviously. Don't you know anything about werewolves?"

Agata sidestepped Lix's next strike, biting off one of his fingers.

She spat it towards Daniel, eyes never leaving Lix.

Panting, he looked from her to those behind her, then back at her, "There aren't enough humans to support you hunting them."

Agata laughed, "You think we'd let those who could be pack die out? We tore the previous zombies to pieces. We drove the vampires back into the shadows until they capitulated to our terms. We forced the elves to hide with the dwarves, their hated enemies. All to keep our to be pack mates alive. You are nothing compared to those threats since you couldn't even attack me from the front."

Lix charged, his eyes enraged.

Dancing aside, her hand slashed up, claws out.

He hit the wall, choked.

Lavender blood spilled out of his cut throat.

She waited out of range as he slumped to the floor, stating, "I fought you face to face. You had no bravery in our previous encounter to do the same, for you are the weak one."

Lix reached back to the old one, his eyes pleading.

The old one looked on without emotion.

She rose to standing, glaring down at her vanquished nightmare, before moving towards him as his body shook from blood loss.

Then she struck with all her speed.

Gripping her prize, she turned to the old one.

Stalking toward him, she watched the others at his sides and back shrink from her.

She held out Lix's head, then dropped it at the old one's feet.

The field holding her shape collapsed as the ship shook, bucked. An explosion thundered in the distance.

The old one locked gazes with her, "What have you done?"

"Giving you the same present you gave humanity when you unleashed your plague," she smirked as fear filled his eyes, "extinction."

She jerked in the support web, shivering from the severed connection to her remote body.

The caretaker tapped her arms, "You are back."

Agata turned to the communication strand, asked, "Daniel? Bron? Doctor Landris? Stefan?"

Stefan laughed, "I know where I rank in the concern order. Alive with a hangover styled migraine."

"I hope there's a cure for this splitting headache," Landris snorted, "And call me Karmal."

Bron's voice sounded strained, "I think I'll just lay here until the lights don't stab my brain."

"I'm here. Kinda lonely being the only one in my head again," Daniel sighed, "Does this mean I can finally be released from quarantine?"

"Ask Lorth," Agata rubbed her temples, trying to alleviate the throbbing growing louder.

"Later," Lorth's voice drew her gaze up.

To the bottle of medicine he offered.

With an appreciative nod, she downed the contents.

"The combined fleets confirmed the bombs have turned the battle," Lorth settled his body lower, "They'll handle it from here."

"They don't need more supernaturals or deities to mop up?" Agata leaned back as the drink eased the throb back a rare knock.

"The Web decided to broadcast your fight with Lix aboard the Breaker flagship. Zinxir are trying to flee from our fleet."

Agata looked at her partner, "They have humans somewhere. I want them back, assuming they don't introduce the plague to them."

"Wouldn't do them any good. While the military worked on the battle, sciences and medical completed the cure. It's being shared."

Agata blinked, tears falling, "It's over."

"This part," Lorth tapped uneasily, "Unfortunately, most of our allies..."

Staring at him a long moment, she dropped her head into her hands, "They think I'm a real werewolf?"

"Alpha Agata Morales, Earth Pack," he confirmed with a bemused tone, "Leader of all supernatural beings from Earth."

Sighing, she shook her head, "I'll deal with this when I've rested."

"You missed two meals," the caretaker interrupted, "Eat first." Giving a low chuckle, Agata took her meal.

Chapter 39

Last Shot

The damn dog faces looked worried.

He blinked past the tears as he watched them gesture furiously, their voices urgent while their words eluded him.

Then they marched towards the birth floor, looking determined and cruel.

Anything would be better news than doing their bidding at this point for their disgusting partners.

He waited for them to reach him, giving his best glare through teary eyes.

Then they all dropped heavily to the floor, their heads separating from their bodies.

Dinner plate sized spiders descended from the ceiling, touching the floor with grace.

"Medicals will be here in an hour," one of them chittered loud enough to rouse the entire room, "Please be patient as we cocoon this area."

His gaze dropped to those spiders collecting vials from the deceased dog faces.

The vile liquid looked sinister to him, even with everything they'd put him through in the months since they took him prisoner.

A shaky voice asked from behind him, "Fam...ily?"

"We'll check once you are in Aqu-jio controlled space."

After what felt like an eternity of waiting, the far doors opened and larger spiders marched in, some bearing medical kits.

When they finally reached him, he wept from his conflicting emotions.

One released his gag, started to ask, "What is your..."

"Take...it...out," he insisted, anger filling him with purpose.

The one who carried over a medical kit to him tapped him, then pulled back, "I would have to take you to surgery."

"No...take...out...like...they...put...in," he felt the pleading entering his voice.

"That would harm you for no reason."

He sent his glare at the spider, "Harm...ing...me...in...side."

The medical paused, then spoke softly, "Please relax."

He gritted his teeth, the endurance he built from all those insertions and 'birthings' letting him stay awake.

The shrieking as the pressure inside eased made him so happy.

"Watch," he panted, looking up at the creepy centipede thing struggling in the grip of the tool he despised above all others.

"Watch?" The spider's confusion showed clearly from its rapidly moving mandibles.

"Watch...it...die," he managed to straighten, his gaze locked on the vile thing he'd been forced to bear.

The centipede's struggles slowed as its voice ebbed, petered out.

Then it hung limp.

"Hold...it...longer," he insisted when the spider went to set it aside, "They...play...dead."

As if understanding its ploy wouldn't work, it thrashed, screaming as it twisted.

The other spider chittered, "Forgot how tenacious the adults are. Didn't realize their young were, too."

Other humans were being led out, moving haltingly with the support of the spiders.

One of the dinner plate spiders joined them as the centipede continued to trashed, "Those will last for months, even at this stage of development."

He growled unhappily, "I...want...it...to...feel...pain...and...die."

"I can bite it if you want it to die in agony. Maybe twenty minutes before it bites the dust as you humans say."

He nodded jerkily, "Yes."

"You sure you don't want it kept in a container to die slowly? Once I bite, we can't undo it."

The thing screamed louder, making his ears ring.

"Kill...it...I...make...choice...now," he panted at the effort just to speak.

The spiders restrained it for the third one.

When the fangs penetrated the centipede, he felt vindicated.

They loosened it so it could flail about, parts of it beginning to swell.

"Die...die...die," he chanted with glee.

His first choice in ages and he'd relish it.

Its chitin split apart, its flesh pulsing out from between the cracks, its screams lessening to choked squeaks.

It twisted, then looked like it was reaching for him, its movements growing weaker.

He recoiled from it in disgust at it seemed to plead with him to save it.

After a long time, it burst from head to tail, splattering its innards on the floor.

He smiled, "Done."

The spiders helped him up, braced him as he shuffled out of the room for the final time.

His last thought on the horrid room behind him focused on the women limping out ahead of him.

The laws used against them were as horrific as what was done to him by the dog faces. He'd insist on those laws being removed from the books immediately.

It was the least he could do to repair the harm they experienced at human hands.

Leaning more on the spiders, he hobbled out to his freedom, happy tears flowing down his face.

Chapter 40
Pursuit

Ziz-ka stood on a new remote drone ship, assisting with the hunt of the Zinxirs as they tried to flee.

Unfortunately for them, enough of their ships had been intact for sciences to scour and figure out the Zinxirs created a short range teleportation system. A system solely reliant on the numerous satellites strewn across their domain to function correctly.

He and his commander were destroying all those satellites so no enemies teleported in behind the waves of ships sweeping deeper into Zinxir territory.

Bron's weary voice commented, "We need to send ships to the other side of the web."

Ziz-ka turned in surprise to face her remote body, "Why?"

"Zinxir ships travelled to those worlds destroyed by their biological weapons some years after they were depopulated. I wouldn't be surprised to find out they had colonies hidden on world, or they evacuated before any other ships came close enough to their colonies to detect them using their teleportation tech."

The commander tapped the communication strand to the Fourth Strand, relayed the standard request for the ranks to listen in.

"The Web is listening," the voices replying before any other.

Once the Master of the Fourth Strand joined them, the commander gestured to Bron.

Bron stood at attention, "Scouts and warships need to go to the worlds devastated by the Zinxir biological weapons. I suspect they have formed colonies on those worlds and used their technology to hide their presence either by masking their location or teleporting away when passing ships moved close enough to scan the world."

"Low Guard of the Web, take charge of this offensive."

"Low Guard of the Web requests the assistance of the remote operators who broke the border ships."

Bron paused a moment, "Two of our number will be unavailable for such tactics. One due to debilitating headaches from prolonged use, the other has been placed back on medical leave."

"Those who are unable to join?" The Web asked.

"Doctor Landris as the former, Chief of Medical Staff Morales as the latter."

"Request Lorth and the Fourth Strand of Medical to join us," the Web spoke softly, "Low Guard of the Web proceed. Missiles will be provided from the factories for your use, should there be a need."

"Chief of Medical Staff Lorth is listening," his tired voice clear before his image displayed his muted demeanor.

"Master of Medical Fourth Strand listening," the Aqu-jio appeared, looking only slightly better than Lorth.

"What can we do to get both Doctor Landris and Chief of Medical Staff Morales prepared for possible remote pico bot usage?"

The Master of the Medical Fourth Strand spoke, "We have a team trying to alleviate pain for Doctor Landris. The programmers believe a minor pathing error lead to her mind being overworked. She most likely will be out of commission until both the pathing is addressed and her mind rested sufficiently."

"Is she resting?" The Web sounded amused, "Our reports from the station have her working with cure teams in the last day."

"I placed her fully with the caretakers. They are cocooning her until she's recovered."

Lorth rubbed his mandibles wearily, "Chief of Medical Staff Morales is taking her scheduled rest period currently. The last remote usage regressed part of her recovery. If she is to take part, remote body connections must be limited to two and three hour segments with rest breaks between for food and sleep periods. She hasn't been cocooned yet, but the caretakers are considering it."

"How bad was the regression?" The Master of Medical Fourth Strand inquired.

"No hissing, thank goodness, but mood swings and trouble sleeping. Facing the Zinxir who nearly killed her is producing mixed results, however the stress symptoms are a little unpredictable with lack of equilibrium for food and sleep still. The caretakers want her kept in her quarters and off-duty for another week, possibly two before reassessing her recovery."

Bron interjected, "Can either of them use a pico bot body if it's at the same location as them?"

Ziz-ka churred in amusement, "What clever idea do you have now?"

"All command decks for the Aqu-jio are identical for ships, stations and bases on worlds. Since they can't come to this deck here, or to one of the ships going to the worlds where Zinxirs could be lurking, why not have the commanders and staff go to the deck for their location via remote body? Then broadcast that deck as if it's the one for the ship. The strain would be considerably less for both of them, assuming either one feels up to. Then we can have Alpha Agata Morales and her Beta Karmal Landris."

Ziz-ka asked, "Why Karmal as Beta or the second in command for this pack, rather than Daniel or yourself?"

Bron smiled, "Bring up the display of our various werewolf forms side by side."

Agata's brown-furred, muscled, towering and massive werewolf form stared out of the screen with piercing yellow eyes and contained aggression.

Daniel's black werewolf form stood taller, but also leaner, less bulky. His silver eyes spoke to great strength and determination.

Bron's silver furred werewolf barely reached Agata's chest. Her form slim, almost delicate yet her features warned enemies to beware her. She would snap their necks as swiftly as a Zinxir while looking on them with her icy blue eyes.

Stefan's tan furred werewolf filled the space around him as if something barely sane lurked behind his yellow eyes, muscles clearly tensed for an attack, lips practically frozen in threatening snarl.

Landris' stood as tall as Agata's, her grey fur clean and neat, which made the scars crossing her muzzle, bisecting her left eye and gnarled her hands stand out the more for how they marred the polished exterior. What could be seen of the bisected eye looked like it was blind white while abyss black blazed with intelligence from the whole eye.

"I'm sure you have advisors who've studied Zinxirs enough to be experts twice over. Ask them who'd they list as ranking in this grouping from the Zinxir perspective."

It took a long moment, which allowed Ziz-ka to look at them as a group.

If he used Aqu-jio rankings, Agata, Daniel and Bron looked equally as leaders, their postures conveying their ability to problem solve as well as fight. Stefan looked like a security member who needed a long rest to recover from some horrendous attack which challenged his sanity. Landris stood as experience, the demoted member to guide the others to promotion.

"Here are the rankings they did individually, then after discussion," the Master of the Fourth Strand stated before the ranks displayed.

All of them agreed Agata was the leader, though each noted different aspects underpinning the outcome, including the obvious will to deal death to those who insulted her or her group.

Landris was second with clear evidence of experience and the ability to fight on in spite of injuries lesser Zinxirs would have been outright killed for, even by their own leader.

The note between Agata and Landris made him rub his mandibles in thought.

These two matched postures, speaking of long standing partnership and unity of purpose. They ruled as one rather than displaying the typical divided positions of other Zinxir groups which eventually led to a death fight between leader and second. Zinxir leader pairs of this nature were recorded as being more difficult to overcome and drove their groups to deeper schemes and higher profits in far less time. One of the Zinxir myths marked one such pair as unbeatable save by extreme old age.

The assessment surprised him since Agata and Landris hadn't been partnered long, if at all.

Daniel was third, his height marked as a known advantage among the Zinxir. The note pertaining to his legs and arms and lack of scars spoke of supreme skill in avoiding hamstringing attacks from fellow Zinxirs.

Stefan was next, his bulk and demeanor of an enforcer or brawler. His words, clipped and almost animalistic marked him as first into a fight. The lack of scars meant his opponents were overcome by his strength and speed before they could land a blow.

Bron was last, too slim and short to be much of a threat. Possible prey.

Ziz-ka chortled, "Well, they would be in for shock since you are clever and quick on your feet. A perfect assassin to get into their blind spot and cut them to pieces."

Bron shook her head, "I saw the way they skipped over me to focus on Landris, Daniel and Stefan instead. They thought me beneath their notice. They really didn't like the way Landris and Agata moved. When Agata stood up to kill Lix, they flicked their gazes between Landris and Agata as if in surprise. They didn't expect something. Most likely they mirrored their postures unconsciously."

The Master of the Science Fourth Strand added a new set of images, "Female humans in sciences and medical have the same posture. Is this some strange training for them to use?"

Bron cocked her head, then laughed, "Look at who they are using it on. Male humans who look to be down talking them. That posture says, you are wrong and I'm going to prove it, so shut up and sit down while I do what I came here for. Military usually trains the posture out of female recruits in favor of them mirroring the males. Conformity to help unity."

Ziz-ka tapped his legs unhappily, "Would you have had that same posture if you hadn't joined your military?"

She shrugged, "Maybe, maybe not. It wouldn't have helped me seem like a bigger threat. Could have detracted from the visual Landris and Agata made."

"The Web wishes both to be made ready. Take what resources you need to make this so, as quickly as safety demands. Agata would be the primary since we can show her fight as a demoralizer once the Zinxir are located."

Bron curtsied as the Aqu-jio lowered their bodies, both in respect. The strand disconnected.

Ziz-ka rubbed his mandibles thoughtfully, "You and Agata understand each other very well. You picked up on her plans without much explanation."

"Only among the Aqu-jio would that be respected. To the Zinxir, that would be expected for lower ranked members so they could survive the orders and whims of their leaders. My weakness compared to Agata's strength."

Ziz-ka loyally countered, "Zinxirs are stupid."

"I agree. I doubt many have seen through the subterfuge Agata put together. They'll believe she is a werewolf even when all the evidence points the other way. All for one simple reason."

The commander asked, "What reason would that be?"

"They don't know humans are flexible enough with the truth to put on costumes and act as entirely different beings. I took a look at the shared strands. Our role-playing games and teaching methods were loaded into the incorrect category."

Ziz-ka hummed as he asked, "Where were they loaded?"

"Archaic practices from before the First Dark Ages. The category states they are not used as of centuries ago or possibly incorrect due to the Second Dark Ages destruction of key information databases and archives," she smiled, "If they had studied it, or not dismissed it, they would have recognized our attack far sooner as fiction wrapped with technology."

Laughing, he turned back to his station, "Let's see how long it takes them to figure it out. I'm hoping the last one gasping curses it as they die."

Chapter 40
Diminishing

Communications from their primary territory made all those in the base tense with anticipation.

Enemies of great power slaughtering security forces as if they were puny prey, their variety in form and powers awe-inspiring. A fight with the Breakers second most accomplished member and his living prey frightened them.

Who knew the humans had Zinxir among them.

No, not Zinxir. Werewolves. Very vindictive werewolves if her words were any clue to her mindset.

The youngest hid in air ducts, staying out from underfoot as the adults prepared for a possible siege, or to hide until the werewolves lost interest.

Warning beacons sounded as multiple ships entered the system.

The leader's ears slowly pinned back as those ships engaged in systematic search patterns. The incoming ships discovered the hole they teleported to, bombarding the location from space until only molten rock remained.

"The Aqu-jio will not allow a second surrender," his mate whispered.

The leader looked up at the screen, cursing the core groups who brought this death on them.

"Sir, we have a communication from the ships," a Zinxir stationed to the side stated cautiously, "I think you need to see it."

The leader barked an order to do so.

Then his ears tried to fold into his skull.

Yellow eyes glared out of the screen, the Zinxir like muzzle displaying the fangs which crunched Lix's nose easily.

"You challenged me for my hunting grounds and dens," the voice growled through the room as if it paced around them, "I accept. Come out and face my pack honorably, or die as my prey."

The leader looked around, seeing postures drooping, whines escaping pursed lips.

Looking at his mate, he made a decision.

He wouldn't allow this werewolf to capture his colony, nor kill them herself.

"Open the line from our side," he forced his ears up, drawing up to face the formidable enemy before him with his pride and courage as shields to the growing dread inside.

"We do not recognize your statements nor rights to harm us. Leave," he ordered firmly and without hint to his trembling will.

Mocking laughter made him flinch, "You struck from the shadows like cowardly rodents. You think we wouldn't rise against you? We had the humans share our stories with all of you as a clear," the bark made everyone jump in fear, "warning not to transgress our territories. You ignored it. Now you face the punishment for it."

On the monitor ships began descending, four missiles like the Aqu-jio breachers flying towards their colony.

He placed his hand on the console, keyed the final resort, "Come dig us out, pathetic human bitch."

Her smirk chilled his blood, "Did you think I intended otherwise?"

Gesturing for the communication to be cut, he watched more ships set up to launch barrages on his colony.

His mate whispered, "Today was supposed to be for joy."

Looking down at her, remembering her words earlier about more children on the way, he bumped his nose to hers, "If those higher in rank hadn't provoked the human werewolves..."

His gaze lifted to the others as they realized there was nothing left for them to do, but to take as many of their enemy with them.

Overloading the teleportation equipment with a command, he counted the ships he'd destroy with them.

Chapter 41
Explosions

Agata gripped the command deck table, shaking as she blinked her eyes, the blinding flare drilling into her head long after the communication line suddenly dropped.

"Ow," she muttered, rubbing a clawed hand carefully over her eye lids.

"Xox-xex Prime and it's surrounding worlds have detonated," Bron blew out a sigh on the other side of the table, "I'm grateful we sent in only drone ships."

Agata requested, "Can we get some polarization on those communications so I don't get blinded on the next one?"

A tap gave her instant relief, removing the spots across her vision.

"That worked," she looked over at Lorth, "Do we have time to get another one in?"

"One more, but then you need to rest," Lorth's mandibles blurred as he rubbed them rapidly with uncertainty, "I never would have thought them suicidal."

Agata wrinkled her muzzle, her tail swishing side to side, "They may have thought by taking out those ships, they could save others. Probably never crossed their minds we have drone ships filled with pico bots instead of real Aqu-jio and humans."

Ziz-ka tapped her shoulder, "I think it was the outfit that made them go out like that."

The Web insisted she should wear an outfit designed to inspire terror in the Zinxir, especially as they added the border ship attacks prior to her fighting Lix to their broadcasts.

Leather patterned after serpent skins on Earth covered her chest like a second skin, edged with snake fangs which clacked as she moved.

Iridescent feathers floated from her shoulders, set in a pattern like those of ranks on a uniform and making up her collar.

A beaded leather loin cloth made her legs look extra long and glittered with iridescent colors to match the feathers.

It borrowed elements of the deity forms Daniel and she took when attacking the border ships.

"If this was all we needed to frighten them, they wouldn't have attacked in the first place," she folded her arms, watching as more worlds were marked as destroyed.

Bron zoomed the view onto a new star system and its group of planets.

"We've pulled back our allies' ships without pico bot remotes on board. They should be out of range, but the longer you can stall them from self-destructing, the greater the buffer," Bron smiled, her werewolf teeth glistening a moment before she hid them again, "Go drive them into our waiting pack members."

She dropped her arms, bristled her fur so she looked bigger and nastier.

"Outer satellites destroyed, inner ones will be removed within thirty seconds," Bron pointed to the ninth planet, "Hidey hole there."

Ziz-ka laughed as it vanished, nearly one half of the planet burning on the display, "Not any longer."

"Incoming communication from the second planet," Bron glanced over.

Agata nodded briskly, staring into the display as if she could see beyond.

The Zinxir had pinned back ears and wide eyes on the screen.

"We have children, please spare us," they pleaded, trying to do a puppy look.

Only Agata could see the calculation behind the facade, undermining their attempt immediately.

"Did you spare any children of the species you infected with a fungal agent?" Agata cocked her head, staring at the Zinxir as if assessing the bones she could break with a bite.

The Zinxir quivered, "You would promote murdering us who didn't harm them?"

She growled, eyes narrowing as her lips pulled back, "You can't say you did them no harm. You took their world, preventing another species of their home from rising into prominence. You purged them, invaded their territory then dare to question me in hunting you down for the same actions against my people?"

The Zinxir seemed to reassess, then stopped cowering, "Come down and fight me one on one, then."

She shook her head, "You have proven weak of spirit. I will allow a fight with a member of my pack to prove my words as truth. Expect them shortly."

Bron cut the transmission, "You sure?"

"Send in a missile with the pico bots. I suspect they'll destroy it or detonate their worlds thinking they killed someone important," Agata sighed, "They are like cockroaches: Survive most attempts to kill them, then when the light is highlighting them, try to run for cover."

The missile didn't reach the world.

The signal stopped as all the worlds and planetary debris exploded.

"Break time," Agata rolled her neck as she strode to the pico bot container.

"Incoming signal from the middle of the Zinxir territory. They want Agata to respond," Bron looked over at Ziz-ka.

"Odd they are asking for me and not the Web," Agata frowned as she walked back.

"The Web is requesting you join their strand."

Agata stood next to Bron and Ziz-ka, "I'll join."

The communication line opened, showing numerous Aqu-jio perched on webs.

She curtsied, stating, "Chief of Medical Staff Agata Morales listening."

"The Zinxir wish to negotiate with you, Agata," the High Guard of the Web spoke respectfully, "The Web wishes to know your thoughts on this."

Agata inhaled, exhaled mastering her lingering fear and burgeoning rage, "Personally, they already exhausted my patience when they forced me to undergo pico bot surgery. I'm biased, heavily against any attempt to negotiate with them."

"Enough bias to play them?"

Agata cocked her head, considered the question, "I'm not already playing them?"

"They want to surrender to you, only you."

Agata felt her teeth bare, "They won't get it, no matter how much they beg. How am I to play them?"

"Slowly cocoon them in their annihilation. While they are attempting to get your favor, you delay them from reacting to our newest forces. Long enough for us to devastate their main worlds."

Agata paced back and forth, rubbing her chin, considering a few approaches and answers then looked at Bron, "I'm not liking the ideas I have on this one. The best I have is setting hideously outrageous conditions on their surrender."

Bron keyed a command as gracefully in her werewolf form as she did in human, "If we use elements of your speech on the Breaker ship, we could make them think there are more survivors of Earth than listed in the strands."

Agata rubbed her head, "The plan you propose?"

"We'll need a few dozen individuals to play beings who haven't been seen yet, and a few others to reprise their roles from before. We'll imply your pack is currently spread out, sniffing out their colonies while the second class citizens under your rule are aiding the main fleets. I think having the Zinxirs become third class under your rule would be enough of a jab to their pride they'll be slow to accept or outright refuse."

"We need your answer shortly. They may decide to detonate their devices and leave a few of our piloted ships in the blast radius," The Web stated.

Agata straightened, "Bron, get our second class citizens organized for a little show and tell. If you need more to play parts, see if Daniel knows where some may be found. Once you have them and they are prepared, we'll open the strand to the Zinxirs."

Time creeped by, making Agata more and more irritated. She wanted just to end it all swiftly.

"Your muzzle is wrinkling," Bron commented as she returned.

Smoothing her muzzle back to a calm demeanor, though she didn't feel it, she looked to the side where Ziz-ka monitored the battle lines.

"You need some set pieces?" An amused voice asked.

Agata turned, sorting the group of individuals who'd joined her, using her medical skills to create her second class citizens.

Stefan acting and visually different compared to his werewolf and human personas smiled so his fangs flashed hungrily, "I heard you may be in need of my brides and I, Lady Morales."

Agata nodded, "I do need my minions."

"Of course. I see we have a few more than our ship incursions."

She wrinkled her nose at the reminder, then glanced at Bron.

Bron gave her the go ahead.

"You have been asked to be background and foundation for a ploy against our enemies. This will require lying about who and what you are. I will need those who are more flexible with truth to move forward."

The Vish-Tarin as a whole slid closer to her, along with a few of the other species, including two Aqu-jio.

"You will be acting as second class citizens to the werewolf pack. Stefan will handle the vampire tie in from my battle on the Breaker ship. Bron, list out those who will be needed."

Bron spoke briskly, "Elves, Dwarves, and two other types of shape changers, which will be were-elk and were-panther. Those are listed in the files the Zinxir accessed. We will also add some others who fall into the deity, monster and immortal categories, though in singles."

"Were-elk?" An Aqu-jio asked with confusion.

"The files have the top three were-creature types as wolf, elk and panther. Hence why we are mirroring it," Bron gestured, "I will recommend the shape changers are treated as the upper second class citizens, all others as lower second class for this effort."

Agata sighed, "I apologize for any misgivings that may result from this lie."

An Aqu-jio raised a leg, "I researched some of your prey animals including the elk. May I be one of were-elks?"

Bron pulled up her tablet, "I have the numbers for each group. I'm marking off one of two were-elks for this presentation."

Grateful for Bron's assistance, between them they allocated everyone a role.

"To ensure this feels more natural, I ask you to assume your roles and we'll go a round or two to get it close," Bron requested.

Agata looked at Bron, "If the Zinxir see you..."

"They won't as I will be something else," Bron transformed into a beefy creature with four tusks and dark brown, leathery skin and large black eyes, her voice turning guttural, "I'm your troll representative."

Bron settled so she stood like a gorilla, knuckles planted on the floor, her muscles rippling with promise.

Agata inhaled, then looked over her assembled non-humans.

They all reacted to the change, many averting eyes and changing postures.

Stefan as Vlad inclined his head with respect, "What do you wish us to do, Lady Morales?"

"Certainly not make any of the Zinxir vampires," she wrinkled her nose, "We have enough issue with recovery without dishonorable ones being made stronger."

"I rather just feast on them. Not as fine bodied as human mind you, but sufficient for the time being," he turned to the were-elks, "How are your newest members? I heard one of them received a bite by one of the zombie-infected."

The were-elk leader snorted, then the high-pitched voice countered, "They are recovered and mended. Do not think we are easy prey like you once did."

"Leader lassie," the dwarf leader called out, "When can we let these ones out of our mines? They'd be best on the surface for clean up after those zombies."

Agata smirked slightly, "Getting a bit crowded down there?"

"Aye," he stated with a grin, "Ye didn't want us digging deeper so we are a wee cramped. At least the pointies don't need ta sleep like us dwarves."

"How could any sleep with your snoring," the elven leader tapped their bow on the floor, tanned skin gleaming with an inner light, "Though I do agree on the overcrowding comment. I hope our performance with this fleet grants us a return to your more benevolent graces, Alpha Agata."

"I'll consider your petition at my leisure," Agata looked at Bron's troll, "I suppose you want to fight in close quarters?"

"Smash good," Bron tossed her head towards the were-elk, "Head butt them also good."

They tweaked a few things, then Agata spoke to the Web, "I am ready to speak to the dishonorable wretches."

She glared at the spot where the Zinxir would appear.

A round table appeared, circled by ten Zinxir.

They pinned back their ears, eyes lowered, postures subservient.

Agata wanted to scoff at their deliberate use of wolf and dog body language.

"Speak," she barked, glaring around the table.

One stood drawing her attention, "I am Rox of the Skinthreads. We wish to surrender to you, Alpha of the Werewolves. Our elders unwisely began these attacks and we wish to make amends for their insults, if you'd allow us."

Agata fought back her instinctive retort, considering the table, then Rox, "How would you make amends for the desolation visited upon my hunting grounds? For the dishonorable treatment of my worlds and those pack mates that will never be mine?"

Another Zinxir spoke up, but kept their eyes on the table, "We are willing to work as manual labor to rebuild your hunting grounds and worlds to their former glory."

"Who are you?" She asked calmly, noting Rox's posture tense slightly.

"Jav of the Boneshards," the Zinxir trembled.

"What else?" She challenged.

Jav peeked up, then back down, the fear in his gaze recognizable, "Else?"

"What else are you offering to address the dishonor?"

A text crossed her vision from the Web, "Keep their attention for at least thirty minutes. More would be appreciated, Alpha."

Rox offered, though he seemed to send a glare at Jav, "All our resources, current and future."

Agata folded her arms across her chest, "And?"

Rox floundered.

Jav leaped on the question, "We will offer up all our planets as your new hunting grounds."

Agata could see the members slowly dividing into two groups. One that tried to hold back reparations, the other willing to do anything to avoid death at all costs, even their pride.

Bron rumbled ominously, "We offer more. They weak. Smash them?"

Agata glanced at Bron, then over to the were-panthers and were-elks, "The Troll speaks truth. All of you offered significantly more for the insult you made when we only lived on one planet."

"Weak. Can't lift loads. Not like us," Bron huffed angrily, "We do more. They useless."

Stefan commented, "I deposited all our funds into your coffers. I gladly parted with such precious gems and coins to be given leniency."

Jav nodded, "We will give you full tithe on any schedule you wish."

Rox smiled, "Would our worlds, our funds and our manual labor suffice as a start?"

Agata didn't like he was attempting to cut off their concessions.

Looking over her gathered team, Agata grinned, "No."

"No?" Both Rox and Jav asked in shock.

Turning back, she pinned all the Zinxir with her gaze, "You are dishonor personified. Your society is built on it, mired by it. You will no longer follow your inferior cultural standards. You will adhere to my," her voice made them flinch, "tenants and laws, just like these have for centuries. Your ways will be forgotten."

Eyes jerked up to meet hers, then dropped as fast.

"You will be fourth class citizens, beneath the humans," she nodded to the others with her, "They are second class citizens. They can command you as surely as any of my pack."

Vlad swept a deep bow, "I will relish the change from lowest of the low."

The dwarves leader replied, "That is a happy change. I look forward to using them for hauling our raw resources to the surface."

Rox's mouth moved up and down, but no sound reached her. Jav and half the table looked relieved.

As if she would allow them to be saved.

"Additionally," she resisted the thrilled smile threatening to take over her face, "I will have my allies, the Aqu-jio, change your pico bots to reduce your self-destructive behaviors, effective immediately. It is obvious your ultra-aggressive urges need to be castrated so you will not threaten others like your elders have for centuries."

Jav whispered, "What else must we do to earn a reprieve from the hunt?"

Agata purred, confident this last one would cause them to break communication, "Your families will be broken up. This will ensure your new behaviors are from those you'll be obeying, rather than any remaining elders or former powers that be."

Rox begged, interrupting Jav, "May we take some time to speak with our brethren so they all agree to your master plan? We wouldn't want anyone to step out of line."

On the heels of request, the Web stated via text, "This may be the best we can do. We'll proceed with our attacks."

"Be aware the longer you linger on your talks, the more of yours will die. My pack will tree your furthest colonies shortly if you don't capitulate to my reasonable demands. With these at my beck and call," she gestured to the non-humans with her, "I will win, regardless of which fate you choose."

Rox dipped his head, "We'll convene it immediately. With your permission?"

She gave him points for the last, but not enough to sway her path, "Go, with my permission."

The strand disconnected.

Bron stated, "We are no longer observed."

Agata looked back at her helpers, "Your assistance played well."

Vlad brushed off his shoulder as if some dust settled on his cloak, "Indeed. I find myself pitying the outcome negotiated will not come to past."

Agata bowed her head, "Thank you for being my strength against them. All of you are appreciated."

Before they could respond Ziz-ka called, "The Zinxirs are firing!"

"Where?" Agata growled.

"At each other," Ziz-ka's mandibles twitched, "No hits on our ships, yet."

Agata watched the displays, wondering what triggered this reaction.

Chapter 42
Dissolution

Rox limped down the corridor of his ship, cursing weaklings like Jav.

As soon as the communication line cut to the bitch, Jav had straightened, "We will live, but we must obey now."

Rox snarled, "Why did you offer so much? We will not be able to recover."

"She was already set to exterminate all of us!" Jav stood bristling his fur in rage, "You didn't see those behind her did you? That brute who looks like it can take on ships with only a suit? This way we live!"

"Live as what?" Rox challenged, "She will strip us of what makes us Zinxir. We'll be dogs to her pack. Sit, roll over, bark. We will never be who we should be."

Jav countered, "We'll live. Even with our families scattered to the stars, we will be alive. We will continue. Nothing changes that we are Zinxir, only our methods. Just like we've done since we killed those early ancestors who were too weak to survive. We feasted on them and lasted. The Alpha will allow us to survive."

"Caged! Branded as her property."

The largest Zinxir blew out a sigh, "Like we did to the humans in our care? If another species did such to us without compensation, we'd have retaliated swiftly and viciously."

"Coward!" Rox snarled.

"She's smart," another stated, "Did you hear how she stated what the hierarchy is? Those who fought her are her seconds, humans third. In our society those humans would have died out. She tended them so they reached the stars. All the while, the presence of these deities, monsters and immortals were nothing more than a story to warn outside the humans. None of the other species forced her into the open, yet she controlled them all. Look at the human laws! They are as strict and constraining as we use for our slaves. She is us, but better. We can learn from her and be more than her pack in time."

"We will be brain dead," Rox snapped.

"We wouldn't have this placed on us if you and your clan hadn't developed the plagues," Jav howled, "You betrayed us all and never thought there was a greater risk in not only attacking the Aqu-jio, but these monsters!"

Rox inhaled to counter, when pain lashed his side.

He backhanded the smaller Zinxir, dislodging the knife from his side.

Chaos reigned, Zinxir attacking each other, some diving under the table, others leaping over it.

He teleported out as three weapons flew towards him.

Coughing, holding his side, he found himself angry at everything and everyone.

The cowardly oldster, the quitters who'd abandoned being Zinxir at the drop of a coin, the Aqu-jio for not revealing the human monsters were real, for the humans who hid monsters as stories.

Entering his bridge, he ordered, "Teleport out."

Sitting down, he pulled the jar of paste to seal his wound.

"We can't teleport."

"What!" His voice filled the bridge with his menace.

"Satellites are not responding. They are reading as in place, but are not functioning. Attempts to restart are failing."

The ship jolted, nearly unseating him.

"Boneshards are firing on us. Jawsnappers are firing on them and us. Returning fire."

Rox stared out at the display in disbelief. Their teleportation network was indomitable. Not even another clan could disable them while leaving the device intact.

"Reports coming in from all over the territory. All clans are warring with each other. Some are begging to take up Alpha Morales' offer."

"That offer is a poisoned pill," he paused the true scope of what she'd done dawning on him, "This is what she wanted. She didn't want us to surrender. She's infected us to kill ourselves."

"A plague?" "How?" "An offer does this?" Voices overlaid each other, panic flowing through his ship.

He stared at the display, "The Aqu-jio are still attacking. They disabled our satellites and sent her in to act as their plague. A verbal plague."

His second looked back, "Is that how she convinced so many to turn on each other?"

"Search their records for anything that can override our wills by verbal or hearing," Rox sealed his wound, clacked his teeth, "We need a counter to it."

"Siren."

"What?"

"A siren is listed as leading sailors to rocks by singing or tricking them into danger," his second looked over, "The only counter is to stuff our ears so we cannot hear the call."

"Order it across all our ships. They must have intentionally split the stories."

"They lied?" His second looked worried.

"She did. She can lie and do it well," Rox felt fear creeping up on him, "She lied about what she truly is. Show us the image of the siren."

The serpentine lower body so close to a snake he could see the truth buried under the disguise Agata used on the border ships.

Even the sketch of the siren mirrored Agata's, down to the look in it eyes as sailors fell from their wrecked ship.

"Get us out of here. All must block their ears and switch to written communications only," Rox ordered.

"Block with what?"

Rox saw the frightful expressions turning to him.

He clenched his fingers, the sound of claws on metal drawing his gaze down.

The sealing paste.

"Use your paste. Quickly! Then get us out of Zinxir space, even if we have to kill the other clans to the last," he turned to his second, "Send out to our colonies to use paste before answering any call of the siren."

His second nodded, hustled to do so.

Shoving the paste into his ears, Rox swore to live through her treachery.

He'd personally see to it she would die under his fangs and claws.

Chapter 43
Intercepted

Ziz-ka opened the strand which didn't register as a real communication, even though it asked for his attention.

"The shadows give this cocoon," the voice whispered, just before data flowed across his vision.

"To the shadows we hope you'll return soon," he relayed the phrase for intense gratitude as he rubbed his mandibles gleefully.

The strand dropped and vanished as stealthily as it connected, leaving the best news.

He walked over to the table, asking for the Web's attention.

Bron who reverted to her werewolf form glanced over before continuing her part in recording the Zinxir's battles.

Agata was at her quarters resting, so he'd have to relay it to her later.

"The Web listens," the weary replied made him happy to deliver good news.

"A data packet came to me that we want to employ immediately."

"What data?" The Web asked.

"One clan of the Zinxir believes Agata isn't just a werewolf, but has the abilities of the Siren monster."

Bron looked over, "Why would they think that? Those are two different monsters."

"They think Agata released a verbal plague which set the battle to rage like a fire. They ordered their colonies to seal their ears and use written communication only when dealing with Agata."

"A verbal plague? How dumb are they?" Bron shook her head, "So they think she's really a siren instead of werewolf."

"No, it gets better," he chittered excitedly, "They think she lied about one of her abilities by planting the story of this ability with a different monster, but left clues since her deity form and the siren picture are both serpentine."

"They know we can lie then," Bron growled, "You should have led with that. They'll be on watch for more lies. If we need a new offensive, we have to account for this discovery."

"Registering explosions at star systems marked for scouting," The Master of the Fourth Strand interjected, "They detonated with half our ships were within the blast radius. Appears to be suicide."

Klaxons blared, jolting all of them.

"Massive explosions in the middle of the Zinxir territory recorded. Ships destroyed being tallied," Bron blinked, "Is this right? The entire Zinxir territory has detonated."

"Military strategists concur," the Master of the Fourth Strand, "Before the detonation occurred, a signal was sent out. Plague containment protocol."

Bron blinked, "They annihilate everything to contain a plague. All but three ships destroyed were remote piloted. Those three piloted register as Aqu-jio."

After a mournful moment, Ziz-ka spoke softly, "I'm grateful for our approach. We only got two groups of humans out before they destroyed their worlds. Our information had one more group deep in their territory."

"We'll need to confirm all those worlds are uninhabitable, before we hunt for their remaining colonies," Bron turned back to her work, typing out orders and plans, "I wouldn't put it past them each clan owned multiple isolated colonies to prevent their species from being wiped out by a single disease. They were using plagues as weapons after all."

The Web ordered, "Implement Lieutenant Commander Bron's plans immediately. If there are any more surrenders, we'll have Agata speak for us."

Ziz-ka looked at the display, wondering how many of those in the shadows just tumbled from the web, forever lost.

"I'll continue fleet maneuvers," Ziz-ka returned to his station, the only thing he could do.

He fought the jolt when another strand that wasn't one connected.

"A new tool is added to the webs of those walking in shadows," the smug voice sent relief though Ziz-ka, before it turned solemn, "with a kill of mercy, and a kill for vengeance."

Replying into the strand only, Ziz-ka inquired, "Oh?"

"You raised me to be smart, demoted partner. Expect us to appear without warning and trigger things left alone."

The disconnected line set his mind at ease.

Obviously his former partner played a part in destroying the Zinxirs as well as evacuating from the area in time. The information of mercy kill meant the humans weren't recoverable.

Peeking at his current partner, he marveled at the strength of such youngsters and what they'd build in the future, even if they had to make agonizing sacrifices to gain peace.

Settling in to do his part, he wondered how Lorth would handle his partner's promotion to a strange and wondrous new role neither had much experience in.

Chapter 44

Cleaned Away

Agata strode into medical for the first time since the Zinxirs destroyed their main worlds, a caretaker shadowing her.

Lorth walked in, guiding a shivering male human out, "I'll schedule a follow-up appointment for your withdrawal symptoms."

The man pointed at Agata, "With her!"

Then he ran out, leaving Lorth tapping in exasperation.

Agata sighed, "I see my brethren are as bigoted as when I left."

"Some are better," he tapped on the console, "That one needs more remedial sessions than I can provide, along with mental assistance."

Agata joined him, looked over the day's schedule, "Aqu-jio only for the rest of your shift."

"If you can manage for me to grab a bite to eat, we can close out this shift together."

Agata looked at the caretaker, got the hum of approval, "Let's go with that plan, Lorth."

He inclined his head, then walked out, his steps light as he headed to the social hexagon.

Familiarizing herself with the next appointments, Agata mentally prepared the list of what she needed to be successful.

Looking up, she smiled at the Aqu-jio who halted at the threshold, "Greetings. Are you here for an appointment?"

"I have to reschedule. I'll send it," he scurried away.

Blinking, she looked down and saw the appointment rescheduled to the next shift.

Rubbing her chin, she reviewed the next appointment.

Bron's voice made her look up.

Ziz-ka tapped his legs nervously as Bron walked in, "This isn't normal."

Agata walked over, "Bron?"

"You recall I asked for advice last month?"

Agata nodded, "Reproduction methods that wouldn't reduce your resources nor decrease your mental acuity. You said you wanted me to be the donor and I agreed."

Bron folded her arms, "Could you check me out?"

Agata shook her head in amusement gesturing towards a private suite, "You went ahead that quickly?

"Yes," Bron smiled, "Unfortunately, I've been having some nausea recently."

"Let's check it out. It could be a slight adjustment is needed," Agata opened the door, waited for Bron to precede her, then looked at Ziz-ka, "You here as family or friend?"

"Worried partner," he tapped her leg, "Please."

"Let him come in. He's probably going to wish soon I hadn't started this, even after he recommended I proceed," Bron groused.

Agata waved him in, then tapped the monitor to switch the front signage to have walk-ins and appointments wait until she returned.

Stepping inside, Agata sealed the room since she'd need the suit on Bron to be disengaged.

"Please pull back your suit from your sides, stomach and back," Agata asked as she brought up Bron's records.

She turned back and then examined the intricate device wrapping Bron's stomach.

Agata checked it over, frowned, "According to what I'm reading, it's operating correctly and the pico bots are not registering any non-standard chemicals for a human pregnancy. Your body is getting the support it needs so it won't steal resources from your other organs. I will need to contact the expert and see if they have a suggestion as to why you are experiencing nausea."

"Please do," Bron folded her arms, "Just my luck, I'd choose the one with problems."

Agata snorted, "Karmal will sympathize with you. She's running two, one is an external incubator, the other attached to her, though in a different configuration than yours. She's having mood swings and worrying the caretakers. She's also been hovering over the incubator to their consternation."

"Worrywart parent?" Bron smiled slightly.

"Between Karmal and the caretakers who are also watching over them, those babies will be cocooned most of the time," Agata straightened, "Our expert is available."

The Hir-zt who appeared grinned at Bron, then Agata, "Well met again. You need help?"

Agata replied, "Yes. Bron is experiencing nausea. We are unable to determine the cause when this method is listed as not having the symptom or eliminating it for those species who do have such symptoms."

"May I look over data? Medical level transfer please," it read the data blinking its eyes in sequence, "Hmm. Strange chemical I've not seen before listed in the recording section about a week ago."

When Agata saw the formula for the drug, she growled, "Not again!"

"You know this?" The Hir-zt gestured with confusion, as Ziz-ka tapped his legs nervously.

"Oh yes," Agata turned to Bron, "Whorish Date."

Bron's eyes turned to steel, "Gregory is still in the brig."

Agata tapped the strand to the station commander and Stefan.

Both appeared, looking baffled.

"Whorish Date, one week ago," Agata snarled.

They glanced at Bron, then back at her.

Stefan smiled as if he could kill by geniality, "We'll deal with it. I'll speak with security and see when it was introduced. Do I need to have a replacement sent up for myself?"

The station commander grumbled, "I'll get next shift on early. I suspect you'll be digging through months of recordings to find them all."

They disconnected, leaving Agata fuming on how to help.

"Whorish Date? What is this chemical?"

Agata replied with the scientific terminology of its impacts on humans.

"Ah, machine operated correctly then. Ingested bad chemicals would cause a nausea to warn user they took in something the machine couldn't handle. It's been decades since it last displayed this warning as species are more careful with food intake."

Agata rubbed her face, "So this was just a warning to watch what she's eating or drinking?"

"Yes, indeed. I've enabled the option that if such occurs again, you'll get a pico bot message stating why the symptom appeared. Any thing else?"

Looking at Bron, Agata cocked her head.

"Can I have this warning at first taste rather than after it's gone through my system? I rather spit it out than throw it up," Bron asked, scowling.

"For some, that would work, but some chemicals react with digestive system processes and can't be detected at the moment of ingestion. I'll have my team work with programmers to add on warning at contact with ingestion point for those we can detect."

They closed out the communication then let it drop.

Agata sighed, began typing out further appointments, "I think you should have caretakers deliver and monitor your food, just like for me. We'll monitor you to ensure neither you nor the fetus are harmed by the drug while you are both at a delicate stage."

Bron gripped Agata's arm, "Could this have harmed them already?"

"We don't have enough information on impacts because of the law. We'll work through it," Agata patted Bron's arm, "You could end up with a very well adjusted child like Daniel."

Bron slumped, "I really want to order everyone to their quarters and isolation until my child is here."

Agata tapped an order for the lab, "Instead of that, we could just have test strips supplied so the bartender can apply them to the sides of drinks and food containers."

Bron perked, "That would mark them immediately."

Ziz-ka chittered unhappily, "We announced those laws were changed. Why are they continuing?"

"Those in power don't change until they are held accountable, either through imprisonment or a change in their circumstances. Maybe we can say the punishment is to be sent to Earth to help with clean-up of all the bodies and cities," Agata finished the instructions for both the lab and bartender.

Before she turned, the bartender had sent a reply she wanted all humans on closed meals until the solution was ready.

"Ziz-ka what would be the best way to get everyone onto sealed meals rather than prepared at the social hexagon?"

He chuckled, "All the Patriot Corp supplied food contains contained more rodent feces than acceptable. The station will provide food from our emergency supplies until a new batch can be created from an allied species. I remember we had that happen a few years ago."

Bron nodded, "Perfect. Except..."

Agata chuckled then pulled out a nutrient pack for humans from medical supplies, "Here. They taste really good since our friends don't want us eating any legs or arms."

"Ha ha," Bron replied dryly, taking the pack, "It's going to take time to get rid of the old ways."

Agata grinned, "I could just order all laws relating to humans are null and void and put the Aqu-jio ones in place. I am the Alpha after all."

Bron snorted, as Ziz-ka considered them.

"I think the Web would appreciate that," Ziz-ka rubbed his mandibles in delight, "Should I get them on the line?"

"If we do it now, I won't regret the decision...much," Agata rubbed her head, "Let me think on it until end of shift, then we'll get us pack members together to discuss pros and cons."

"If you rush it, you'd be the designated law judge," Bron gave a beautiful grin, "and when would this child ever see you?"

Agata laughed, "I made time for Daniel. If any of the children bearing my DNA needs me, I'll make the time."

Bron smirked, "So who else?"

"I don't follow," Agata frowned, trying to figure out the real question.

"Daniel, this one," Bron patted the device, "who else has your DNA?"

Agata grinned, "None at this time, but I may want another in the future. Some of the reproduction methods looked intriguing, but I would need help raising them so I don't end up in a bad state again."

"Who would you want to donate to your child?"

"I don't know. I may just randomly pick one of the samples from the warehouse no one else chose," she shrugged, "It won't happen until I'm fully released from the caretakers. You can reinstate your suit. I think we've done all we can this session."

With the appointment finished, Agata escorted them both out to the main area.

Three Aqu-jio waited, chatting.

"Thanks, Agata," Bron strode out, Ziz-ka lowering his body to Agata briefly before catching up to this partner.

Agata turned to the waiting Aqu-jio, "Pardon for the wait. May I ask who has an appointment?"

They stared at her a long moment, then each other.

"Just was going to chat with Lorth on some medical news he might find interesting," one offered with a nervous mandible rub, "I can come back when it's less busy."

Agata blinked as two of the three left.

Turning to the security Aqu-jio she asked, "Do you have an appointment?"

"Yes, Alpha."

Agata rubbed her temple at the tension she noted in the legs and mandibles, "I take it you would prefer Lorth to handle your appointment, yes?"

"Please, Alpha."

Agata turned and looked over the schedule.

Only one remained for Lorth's shift. Confused by the odd changes she noted the appointment wanted an Aqu-jio attending.

"Lorth should return shortly. Do you need anything while you wait, like medical information for review?"

"No, Alpha," the security Aqu-jio settled in the corner.

She reviewed the inventory and sent in requests for resupply and additional items so Lorth wouldn't have to do it when he returned.

By the time Lorth returned, she had completed all the tedious tasks and required documentation.

He stepped in, glanced at the security Aqu-jio with surprise, "Are you waiting for me?"

"Yes!" The Aqu-jio tapped his legs happily, "Please."

"Agata, do you need a break before I attend to his appointment?"

"I don't need it. He's been waiting a while," she replied.

Lorth escorted the Aqu-jio into the back.

Agata checked the remote medical check-ins, saw none for several weeks. With the lifting of the containment, medicals could move freely again. Reducing the need for remote medical time.

She looked up at a polite high-pitched chirr, "Greetings to medicals?"

Agata didn't see any Aqu-jio immediately.

"Greetings," Agata came around the console.

On the ground was a frail looking, bright orange and green female Aqu-jio who matched the size of the spider plushie in her quarters. Something about the color tickled a memory.

"Chief Medical Agata of Morales via Human Prime," the Aqu-jio greeted politely, "Is there an opening for an on station physical?"

"Of course. Would you like to wait for my partner or would you like me to handle it?"

"You. My ship is docked only for a limited time."

"This way, please," she walked so the Aqu-jio could scurry beside her.

"The last human to see me took several minutes to locate me," the Aqu-jio commented.

"One of my first patients was an Aqu-jio near your size. I try to make sure to look down and around. Several of my patients prefer ceilings over floors and walls."

The Aqu-jio climbed the table to stand on top as Agata closed the door, then pulled up records.

"I see you are due for a vaccination next week. Would you like that now, or held until your next physical?"

"Now," the Aqu-jio settled, watching with all her eyes, "If you can also add the next one, that would be preferred."

"The second one would be right after your next physical. Are you anticipating being unable to attend that timing? I can make a note if that helps."

"You are not what I expected."

Agata turned at the non-sequitur, "In a good way?"

"For a werewolf and leader of immortals, maybe."

Several connections formed in her mind, and she groaned, "Is that why all the Aqu-jio are avoiding me? Because they think I'm a werewolf."

The amused chirr made her look over at the Aqu-jio, "You performed well with that part. Would you be willing to do it again?"

"I heard most Zinxir colonies were located based on information found on one of their ships. Why would I be needed again?" Agata wanted to wince at the implication.

The gaze of the Aqu-jio seemed to peer deep into her, "There are other species out there who could be frightened into better behavior by the fearsome werewolf Alpha of Human Prime and lessen some duties those of us perform."

"Who are you?" Agata inquired feeling as if she was adrift in space.

The Aqu-jio assumed a formal posture, "High Guard of the Web Kioxiz of the Flaresingers via Aqu-jio Second."

It clicked then. At the first meeting of humans and Aqu-jio, this one requested information for the Web on the Fourth Strand to check the science report.

The mandibles rubbed, "You recognize the name, yes?"

She nodded numbly, "I wouldn't have expected someone of your rank to visit a station for something as mundane as a physical."

An amused hum, "This serves two purposes. One to get my check-up out of the way by someone who is known for kind attention on vaccinations. The second to see if you are willing to play the role for a longer time in defense of our shared web."

Agata rubbed her nape uncertainly, "I can attend to the first readily. The second, I'm going to have to think on."

"Please proceed with the vaccinations," Kioxiz settled comfortably.

She pulled up the two vaccinations, checking them off inventory, then onto the records for Kioxiz, noting the request for early vaccinations.

She turned and requested a leg where the vaccination would start from and for the suit to be pulled away.

Gently bracing the thin leg with two fingers, she touched the vaccine to the leg just below the joint.

Kioxiz waited as the vaccine slowly entered her system.

When the first was done, Agata asked, "Would you like the second on the same leg?"

"Please."

Setting aside the first container, she picked up the second and started the process again.

When finished, she straightened, "You can let your suit settle over the space again. You may experience some joint pain since you received two at once. If it becomes persistent or more severe, please consult a medical immediately."

Collecting the used vaccines, she deposited them into the box where they'd be cleaned and reused.

"Well worth the side trip for just the vaccines," Kioxiz stated, drawing Agata's attention, "What are your thoughts on my offer?"

Agata spoke calmly, "I took up the role as I...to be honest, I loathe the Zinxirs so much that if I had the power to clap my hands and instantly kill them all, I would do it in a heartbeat. I may not be the best person to be introduced to species that only need a light touch to convince them to behave."

"I'm not asking for your aid on those cases. These would be species much like the Zinxir. Ultra-aggressive is how you put it. They may lie or tell the truth, but they need to be faced with something as aggressive and powerful as Alpha Agata Morales, leader of the immortals, deities and monsters from Human Prime. One who subjugated beings of immense power and who can tear apart a space ship in minutes when called upon. If they don't respect or back down from you, we would be more in a position to handle them better than the Zinxir."

"As in the same destruction?" She asked, dreading having to wipe out more species.

How would that make her any better than the Zinxir?

"Containment first, annihilation last," Kioxiz replied with the same weariness Agata held, "I do not relish nor seek the end of any species, but there are some that cannot coexist with us and those we have treaties with. We have a responsibility to protect them from the web-shredders and flames threatening our peace."

"Is this something the Web endorses?" she asked.

"There are those who walk in the shadows to keep us safe. They make some of the terrible decisions and bear guilty burdens, like triggering a plague containment for a species to destroy the bulk of them and sacrificing a few for thousandfold more. I am one of those who can call upon them for their skills, along with two of the Web."

Agata covered her face at what Kioxiz implied and outright stated.

Looking at the floor, Agata considered the offer, searching for the answer her heart and mind could live with.

"How often would you be calling upon me and those who'd join me to play boogymen to these other species?"

"Others?" Kioxiz paused.

Agata shook her head, "If I do this, my entire pack has to be part of it. The others who helped may need to join as well. The more impressive and solid the lie, the less likely anyone would question it."

"I hadn't thought of needing all. I hoped only one would be enough," Kioxiz tapped her legs on the table, "I will need to ponder on your counter proposal."

Agata closed her eyes tightly, then blew out a breath, opened them again, "If you need me, I'll be there."

"It's the opening of our negotiations," Kioxiz leapt easily to the floor, moved with grace and power towards the door, "I think the next session will be easier when I know if we want this to be more of a group rather than an individual helping us."

Agata followed, heading back to the waiting area, then frowned, "Why am I better at vaccines? I learned from Lorth how to do them and he taught it off the standards."

She stepped into the waiting area then looked up at the biggest Aqu-jio she'd ever met. The female filled the space such no one could pass her if she crawled through the corridor.

Lorth rubbed his mandibles nervously, easing backwards, as the new Aqu-jio made a low level hiss.

Agata blinked as the towering Aqu-jio moved towards her.

"We need to conference," the female rumbled in a deep voice, continuing to hiss angrily.

"If we do so, we should do it over a proper meal. Lest the caretakers intervene," Agata nodded to the slowly rising caretaker, "I also think having us get into a fight would cause a stir that may cause the males to abandon the station."

"You don't know who I am," the Aqu-jio accused.

Agata politely replied, "We have not been properly introduced. Chief of Medical Staff Agata of Morales via Human Prime," remembering Kioxiz's comments regarding her infamy, she appended, "Alpha of the werewolves and leader of the immortals."

"The Web, sector seven," the Aqu-jio leaned closer, "The Web in charge of Medical and First Contact."

Agata glanced at Kioxiz sitting under a console, mandibles moving as if in silent amusement.

"Then a conference is critical. I think Kioxiz should join us as well."

Kioxiz froze as the Web stopped hissing.

Agata continued, "Obviously, something in the procedure for vaccines as handled by me is different than how Lorth does them. As vaccines are critical to health of all Aqu-jio, we need to ensure the ease of their administration. I have the impression Kioxiz can offer insights into the differences."

The Web's mandibles rubbed slowly, "Your social hexagon should have the appropriate space for such a meeting."

"I agree. It also helps we'll be near food and drink as needed while we have this conference for a variety of topics."

The Web moved backwards, then made her way towards the social hexagon.

Lorth asked, "Do I need to call the next shift?"

Agata looked down at Kioxiz, considering what hot water she'd been dumped into, "I think you should stay here and clearly post I'm not on shift. The rescheduled appointments earlier may be because of who I am. Perhaps new signage including when last I ate would help."

Lorth nervously tapped his legs, "Do you want to take a nutritional container?"

"Yes," Agata gestured after the Web had gone with a smile, "After you, Kioxiz."

"Medicals are crazy," Kioxiz muttered then scurried out as Lorth set the container next to Agata.

"Security is clearing the social hexagon," Lorth sighed, "I hoped we'd be back to our normal shifts again."

Agata hefted the container, replied, "I doubt any human will be back to normal shifts for some time, Lorth. You may need to send a second container in a little while."

"I'm glad you noticed it," Lorth sank, "I wonder how soon she'll be laying her eggs."

"Can you check with their ship and ensure she's not forced to scrunch through any corridors? I don't think anyone on that ship would be happy if she found herself stuck."

Lorth cursed, "On it."

Agata left to calm down an angry female Aqu-jio, then figure out why Kioxiz dared to tick her off. She had the feeling the vaccinations she administered should have been done by the Web for Kioxiz.

Chapter 45

Last Contact

Bron walked towards the open doors of the colony, her steps brisk.

Fifty years had passed too fast for her.

At the suggestion of the Aqu-jio she'd taken on a new form forty years before.

Muscle circled her arms with the potential to crush her enemies, her claws long and deadly even when she was at ease, ears tall with tufts of golden fur.

No scar on her body as her space black fur danced in the breeze flowing from the entrance.

Entering with confidence and arrogance, she sniffed the air.

It stank of death and sickness.

She encountered her first body just beyond the light the doors let in.

Zinxir, and long deceased.

Lips pulling back from her teeth, the serrated edges a sign to any Zinxir she was a Deatheye, a mythical being the Zinxir would see as they crossed over into death.

Her glowing white eyes scanned, showing as both the white of death and the white of something beyond death, she descended into the depths of the colony.

Young, old, weak, strong lay where they fell. None had been spared.

The latest species to join the web, the Liritotz, had cowered from Agata at a medical meeting, begging not to be harmed by the one who brought death. They did it to her human form, not her imposing werewolf form.

It took six months of assuring the Liritotz Agata wasn't hunting them to coax them back to the treaty table. Another two months to find out one of their colonizing ships escaped a Zinxir world with all mortally wounded but a few of their youngsters.

Bron was sent to strike fear into the Zinxir before their worlds would be destroyed, by either side.

Except everywhere she searched methodically contained the same scene: dead bodies decomposing into rotting messes.

Wondering if this would be the last Zinxir colony she'd get the chance to see, Bron slid through an open door.

Into the command deck of the colony.

The ever prevalent round table, a perversion of the ancient mythos of great knights from her home world, stood covered in layers of dust and debris.

A noise made her slowly turn, the motion detailed down to the ear turn to mirror the horror stories of the Zinxir.

Sitting in a chair, the Zinxir coughed weakly.

"So you have come for the last of us, Deatheye?"

Bron silently stalked the Zinxir, dialing up her glowing eyes until they were like flashlights. Spotlighting the Zinxir calmly sitting as if she had no more energy to move.

"When the last beacon vanished twenty-nine years ago, we knew we were the last in the entire universe," she coughed, spitting out white, "Why did the Deathsiren call for us so slowly when many disappeared swiftly in those early years?"

Kneeling, jerking her head to the side, cracking her spine, Bron stared at the Zinxir silently.

"I was born as the Deathsiren started her attack. Born only to die. Why was I brought into this world only to live in agony? To never hear anything, to be left alone screaming for help yet none looked for me. To claw my way out of the darkness, only to be tossed back down."

Bron read the text from Ziz-ka, "This one didn't jerk at your neck crack. With the last comment, she may not be able to hear it. Shift so you can look at her ears."

Directing invisible pico bots to the side, she waited a second. Then she switched which ones were visible, making it appear as if she jerked to the side, crouching in a different position.

Strangely, the Zinxir's ears were blocked with some unnatural looking skin.

"When they finally gave me the written word link, it was the only happiness in my life," she hacked, more white spraying out, "I could understand and be understood."

Ziz-ka's softened voice stated, "Medical says it's most likely the paste Zinxir's used to seal their wounds. The strategists think they heard the last communication about plugging their ears if they talked with Agata to mean to block their ears immediately."

Bron blinked slowly, a very tiny part of her sorry for the child who'd suffered all for a communication snafu.

Pushing it aside, she texted back to Ziz-ka, "Quick death?"

"No, but we can share the truth finally. Their computers register there are no more colonies. This is the final colony we needed to find, and she is last of them according to our scans. Here's what medical recommends."

Standing, Bron stalked smoothly to the Zinxir.

Her eyes widened, "This is the end?"

Placing her hands over the ears, the pico bots opened the way into the ear canal, removing the built up wax.

Moving back, Bron looked at the startled Zinxir.

"Can you hear me?" Bron spoke with icy calm.

"Yes," the Zinxir glanced over as a computer whirred to life, lights turning on through the room, "I never imagined it would sound like that."

"Your species committed grave offenses against others," Bron stated, "You are the last. You deserve to know all the reasons your people have died out."

Bron listed every species, and the total lost lives, dispassionately watching the Zinxir's ears lower with each world and planet.

When Bron completed with humanity, the Zinxirs ears were pinned to her head, "Do you understand now?"

"Who is the Deathsiren? Who summoned her?" A rattle echoed in the room.

Agata's voice filled the room, "I am the Deathsiren."

Bron watched the Zinxir look up at Agata's werewolf form in confusion, "You are one of us."

"No. I am human. A human using pico bots to present this disguise."

Bron watched the truth sink home as Agata took her human form, intentionally showing the pico bot swarm before reforming.

The Zinxir looked at Bron, "Deatheye?"

Bron switched to her human form, looking down on the last of the terrible race, "Another human. We used your stories, your myths against you."

"That is why we suffered," the Zinxir hacked, globs of white oozing out of her mouth, "We attacked a race more Zinxir than we were."

A wrinkle crossed her muzzle then she asked, "Why give me my hearing?"

Agata sighed, "So you can tell the rest of the Zinxir what destroyed them. It wasn't the humans, the Aqu-jio, monsters, immortals nor deities. It was the Zinxir themselves. They thought so little of others, destroyed them at a whim, cackled when they wiped out entire worlds, that when their actions came to light, they had no defense against their reflections."

"I don't understand," the Zinxir blinked.

"When you harm those around you, that harm comes back onto you eventually. The harm was five centuries in coming back to your species. It's why in your final years, you hid deep and took away your own hearing."

"But it wasn't you who killed us. It was the sickness."

Agata nodded, "The Liritotz, those antlered beings like this," her form changed to a centaur like elk with blunt fingers, "You attacked them."

"Yes. Only a few escaped. We ate those we brought down."

"When one of them dies through anything but old age, their bodies release multiple pathogens. Viruses, bacteria, fungi and a plethora of others that turn their bodies into plague carriers. You ate the very thing that killed you. If you could have heard them, you would have heard their warnings to not eat them, that they carried death inside them."

The Zinxir smiled bitterly, "It came back unto us. Everything..."

She jerked, choking as white oozed from her mouth.

Bron watched with Agata as the last Zinxir expired.

"They didn't care about their own children enough to ensure they had a future," Agata stepped forward, closed the eyes of the corpse, "If they had, they would know symbiosis is better in the long run than parasitism."

Bron exhaled, "I don't have to be the last thing they see anymore."

Agata gripped her shoulder, "In time the nightmares they spread will be nothing more than stories. They will be the myths that warn others not to act the same."

"Did they leave any plagues in their labs?" Bron asked.

"They did. Let's go deal with them so there are no weapons left to destroy others," Agata walked away.

Bron joined her, walking back towards the labs, silent for a long while.

"We would have been just as bad as them."

Agata looked over, nodded, "Patriot Corp and those like them would have lead us to the same end. In a way, the Zinxirs helped us by killing those off who were parasites onto their own kind. Now we can look to the stars and be symbiotic with the web."

"I want to go cuddle with our grand children," Bron's shoulders slumped, "This has been a bitch to finish."

Agata nodded as she began denaturing the plagues, "Tomorrow we focus on better projects. Adding strands to this web until it spans every galaxy, and lasts to the end of time."

Bron closed her eyes, smiled sadly, "I think I need a vacation first. This one got to me."

"I know. She was born at the eve of her species downfall. She hadn't done anything to deserve it," Agata blinked her eyes, holding back tears, "neither had any of the babies and children on Earth and our colonies deserved agonizing death so soon into their lives. Death suffered at the hands of those who should have protected them."

"At least good people stood up to face the enemy," Bron exhaled, "Just wish there were more of our survivors."

"Humanity needs more maturity to let go of those barbaric customs. I have faith they will reach it sooner than later. Those who have more maturity can build thriving families, unlike those mired in natural birth and other anachronisms."

Bron paused a moment, recalling something she saw earlier in the day.

Chuckling she asked Agata, "Did you see the video of Gregory's grandson when he was told he'd have to carry his own offspring if he wanted any? He looked like he'd been hit with a ship at the end of his trial."

"Lorth and Ziz-ka both have strange and sick senses of humor," Agata shook her head, "I still don't understand how they convinced the Web in their entirety to set that as the punishment for men using Whorish Date."

"Or women have to donate to the warehouse and hope someone else wants to use their DNA for children if they do the same?"

"That wasn't Lorth, nor Ziz-ka."

Bron looked over at Agata, "Oh?"

Agata winced, "That was from the Web, sector seven, Kioxiz, and I talking a few decades ago."

Bron leaned in, "There's a story there."

Agata muttered, "I'm not commenting on this."

Bron thought back through the years, then straightened, "Was this when you and them ended up in the caretaker's section under full cocoon?"

Agata sighed, "The dock worker should have kept his mouth shut. She would have been on her ship and off our station, but for his stupidity. A human had no right to call her fat."

Bron grinned, "At least we got something out of it."

"We did?" Agata finished, stepping back.

"Hangry female drills."

"That's why those drills started?" Agata shook her head, "I thought it was because of my hissing."

"I know what bedtime story to tell to the new babies," Bron walked out of the labs.

Agata groused, "Just record it this time. I don't want to hear Lorth, Ziz-ka, nor Stefan whining about missing it."

Bron laughed, her voice echoing through the colony, chasing the ghosts away.

About the Author

The author co-habitats with multiple, overburdened bookcases.

With twenty years of writing as a hobby, gleefully coaxing friends and family to review each new story, the author continues to add books to the collection for readers to enjoy.

www.ingramcontent.com/pod-product-compliance
Lightning Source LLC
Chambersburg PA
CBHW020836260626
47169CB00003B/1011